I0590568

CONCIERGE
AFFAIRS

VALERIE WILCOX

Black Rose Writing | Texas

ISBN: 978-1-68433-501-5
PUBLISHED BY BLACK ROSE WRITING
www.blackrosewriting.com

Printed in the United States of America
Suggested Retail Price (SRP) $18.95

Concierge Affairs is printed in Baskerville

*As a planet-friendly publisher, Black Rose Writing does its best to eliminate unnecessary waste to reduce paper usage and energy costs, while never compromising the reading experience. As a result, the final word count vs. page count may not meet common expectations.

In memory of David H. Wilcox

Together for 37 years and forever in my heart.

ACKNOWLEDGMENTS

The person I most want to thank will never read these words. When Dave died in 2019, I lost more than a loving husband. I lost my first reader, my computer expert, my technical advisor, my biggest fan, my cheerleader, and my source of never-ending support and encouragement. He was a brilliant engineer but spelling sometimes eluded him. He made a screen saver affirmation for me when I started writing my first novel and needed a boost to keep going. It said: *I Am A Great Writter*. I may never be a great writter or writer, but Dave believed in me and for that I will always be grateful. Special thanks go to Rita Gardner, John Wilcox, and Beth Schliehert for their unique contributions. And, of course, a big thank you to all my friends, relatives and other readers who continue to support my writing career. I couldn't do it without each of you.

CONCIERGE

AFFAIRS

CHAPTER ONE

KATE

"Woman Falls from Sky – Narrowly Misses Bystander" was the headline in the *Seattle Times* article that covered the suicide of Marie Talbot. It was a creative attention-grabber, but the report had little resemblance to actual events. I know. I was the so-called bystander.

First, Marie didn't fall from the sky; she fell from the roof of a twenty-story apartment building. Second, she didn't commit suicide; she was murdered, pushed to her death by person or persons unknown. Third, her name wasn't Marie Talbot; she was christened Marija Trstenjak, and although she'd never legally changed her given name, she'd dropped it as soon as she turned eighteen. And finally, I wasn't just standing by on the sidewalk waiting for her body to tumble out of the sky and land in a heap right in front of me; I was on my way to a meeting with Marie at my ex-husband's office.

At the time, I didn't know all these details. I didn't even know that it was Marie Talbot who had plunged headfirst off the building. All I could focus on then was how broken the woman's body looked--legs twisted and crumpled, neck and head crushed, both arms cruelly torn from their sockets. She had apparently stretched her arms out in front of her on the way down as if they could somehow cushion the impact. They didn't. There was surprisingly little blood at first, but within seconds she was bathed in a gruesome pool of red. For some odd reason, I was struck by how the afternoon sun brought out the blond highlights in her hair—that is, until they became nothing more than sticky-looking dark red streaks. I turned my head away from the grisly scene, but I couldn't avoid the fact that I was smack-dab in the middle of this tragedy. And I was probably going to be late for my meeting.

It was a meeting I hadn't wanted to attend in the first place. I'd never met Marie Talbot and wasn't pleased that I'd let my ex-husband coerce me into agreeing to do so. I'd told Jack when he called that I didn't want to get involved with his clients. He owned Doyle's Private Investigations and somehow thought I was his partner. I was no such thing. I ran my own business—Premier Concierge Services—and didn't need any distractions—least of all from my ex-husband. But Jack was insistent.

"We used to be a damn good team once upon a time."

"You just don't get it," I told him. "We're not married any more. That's what the *ex* in ex-husband means." We'd been together for over twenty years and it had been several years since our divorce. Jack had been married and divorced again in the interim and his second former wife apparently had better sense than to answer his phone calls.

"Don't think of me as your ex-husband," Jack said. "Think of me as an investigator who needs your expertise."

"And just exactly what expertise would that be?"

"Let's not get into all that right now. Just say you'll meet with us."

"I can't, Jack. I don't have any time to spare." I'd just inked a new contract for concierge services at a condominium in a wealthy Seattle suburb. It was something of a coup that my fledgling business won the contract and I was determined to succeed. I explained all this to Jack, but he wasn't the type to be put off easily.

"Just this once. Meet with Marie and me one time. That's all. Then you can go back to whatever you have to do. Please, Katie."

My name is Mary Kathleen Ryan, but most people know me as Kate. When Jack started calling me Katie, I knew he was desperate. Jack liked to project a macho vibe, but he had a vulnerable side that he tried to keep at bay—usually with too much alcohol. He'd been semi-sober for a while now but getting booted out of the Bellevue Police Department had done a number on him. It seemed to me that he was close to the edge again—which is probably what he was counting on. My weakness has always been bad boys in trouble. And Jack knew it. Once again, he'd played me.

"Okay," I sighed. "One meeting. I have to be in Seattle to see my accountant, so I guess I could swing by for a few minutes first."

"That's my girl! Meet us at Java Joe's."

Short on funds, Jack couldn't afford a regular office. He called the coffee shop next door to his apartment building his "office" and conducted all his business at a corner table there. The business, so far, mainly consisted of working the phone to drum up referrals from his former colleagues and all the lawyers he used to call scumbags, who'd still take his calls. I suspected that that was how he'd snagged Marie Talbot as a client, but it didn't matter. I'd meet her as promised, give whatever expertise I could to help Jack out, and then get on with the rest of my day.

The neighborhood where Marie's life ended wasn't the best Seattle had to offer, but it had great character—and great characters, as Jack often joked. The city's guidebooks said it was "in transition," which was a nicer way of saying "less desirable." No upscale shoppers, dressed-for-success types, or tourists need apply here. Nevertheless, a woman's screams as she fell twenty stories to her death attracted a lot of attention from the upwardly mobile and downtrodden alike.

Someone in the mixed crowd that had gathered to gawk at Marie's shattered body had evidently called 9-1-1. The sirens wailing in the distance jolted me out of my dazed state. I'd just eased away from the onlookers when I spotted Jack sprinting down the sidewalk toward me.

"Kate!" he shouted. "Wait up!" Although he'd missed the woman's actual fall, word about it had quickly spread to the coffee shop. Most of Java Joe's patrons now milled about with the rest of the throng.

I leaned against the fender of a nearby parked car. "She was only wearing one sandal," I mumbled as Jack approached.

"What?" he asked, struggling to catch his breath. Jack and physical exertion were not on the best of terms. His six-foot-two frame was still muscular, but he'd put on a few pounds around the middle lately. Not that he'd ever admit it. Turning forty-five a few months ago was hard enough for him to accept.

"A bright red Jimmy Choo," I said.

His dark blue eyes locked on mine, clearly concerned. "Are you all right?" he asked.

"I wonder where her other sandal is," I said, scanning the sidewalk for the wayward footwear.

Jack pulled a handkerchief from his suit pocket and gently wiped my face. I'd been so stunned when Marie hit the pavement that I hadn't realized some of her blood had splattered onto my face and suit. Jack fussed over me until I brushed his hand away. "I'm fine," I said.

"Are you sure?"

Maybe not. I'd begun to shiver even though it was a hot August afternoon which, for Seattle, was a scorching 75 degrees. An ambulance pulled up alongside the curb, followed by two police cars. The medics barreled through the crowd to aid the victim who was beyond help while two uniformed officers barked orders to the curiosity seekers to disperse.

"Okay, Katie," Jack said, taking off his suit jacket to wrap around my trembling shoulders. "We need to get you out of here." When he was still working for the BPD, Jack never cared much for what he wore. Let's put it this way: he was a walking cliché--a rumpled Columbo-like homicide detective with just enough Irish bravado to make it work. Someone must have convinced him that a professional image was important when you ran your own business. The jacket he'd given me was Brooks Brothers and the smart look he now favored also included a crisp white shirt, silk tie, and spit-and-polish Florsheim's. He was dressed to impress Marie Talbot.

"I don't think I'm up to meeting your client right now," I said.

"Marie never showed," Jack said. "I guess we'll have to make it another day."

"Hey, Doyle!" The shout came from one of the uniformed officers. "You got a minute?"

"I've gotta see what this guy wants," Jack said. "I'll be right back." Although he had spent the latter part of his career as a homicide detective in the suburbs, it wasn't surprising that Jack was recognized by Seattle's uniformed rank and file, especially since he'd been brashly marketing his new business to anyone in the precincts who came within spitting distance of him.

While he was gone, I took some deep breaths to get my nerves under control. I was beginning to feel more like myself again when Jack trotted back to the car a few minutes later. He ran a hand through his thick, but neatly trimmed "do" and frowned. There was more gray than black in his hair these days which, frankly, I found appealing. That anything about Jack still appealed to me after all these years was annoying.

When I saw his pale and sweaty face, I realized that the unflappable Jack was visibly shaken. As horrible as the woman's bloodied and broken body was, I knew he'd probably seen worse in his day. "What's wrong?" I asked.

"I need a drink."

Jack was a case study in classic conditioning. He automatically turned to alcohol whenever he felt distressed and it irritated the hell out of me. "Get a grip, Jack. If you think a dead body is bad, try having it almost land on top of your head."

Jack paused, struggling to breathe. "It's Marie Talbot, my new client," he gasped.

"Oh, Jack, I'm so sorry." I linked my arm in his. "About that drink," I said. "What did you have in mind?"

CHAPTER TWO

JACK

I recognized Marie Talbot as soon as the beat cop called me over to look at her crumpled body. She had on the same flowered sundress that she'd worn when I first met her. The silky fabric was a bloody mess now, but two days ago it had wrapped around the sensual curves of her body like a warm embrace. I couldn't believe as I looked at her broken and battered legs that I'd ever mistaken her for a dancer. I averted my eyes from the mangled heap that had once been a vibrant young college student and crossed myself. "Jesus, Mary, and Joseph," I said. "It's Marie."

"You know the jumper?" asked the officer.

She hadn't smiled much during our first meeting, but when she did—wow! Sparkling blue eyes, straight white teeth, and full lips accented by deep dimples in both cheeks were a dazzling combination. Marie wore bright red lipstick and very little other makeup. She had no need. Marie Talbot was one of those women who possessed a rare combination of womanly beauty and youthful naiveté—innocent and sophisticated at the same time. There was something else, something vaguely familiar about her that made me ask whether we'd met before. She assured me we hadn't, but I couldn't shake the feeling that we had. Officer Fitzgibbons didn't need to know all that. He just wanted her ID confirmed. "What about it?" he asked again. "Do you know her or not?"

I could have told Fitzgibbons right away that I knew Marie Talbot. But my career as a homicide detective for over fifteen years taught me a lot. I could have told him she was just a young farm girl from Yakima, but smart enough to know that she was in trouble. I could have told him she was scared out of her wits but jumping off a twenty-story building wasn't how she'd deal with her problems. I could have told him a lot more but what I said was, "Should I know her?"

"You tell me," Fitzgibbons said, waving a blood-stained card in my face. "She had your business card on her." I'd always figured Fitz for a snarky ass and he didn't disappoint. "Finally got yourself a client, huh?" he snickered. "Hope you got a retainer up front."

I wanted to take the guy down a peg and would have if I'd still been on the force. But I needed all the contacts I could get now, snarky asses or not, and let his petty jab go. "She's Marie Talbot," I said. "A sophomore at the University of Washington."

"Why'd she hire you?"

"Sorry. That's privileged."

He looked at me with an expression I knew well; it was the same disgusted scowl that I'd flashed over the years whenever some legal eagle dodged my questions. Now that the shoe was on the other foot, I found the tactic useful and more than a little satisfying. I took off before Fitz could press me further.

My hasty retreat had nothing to do with avoiding unwanted questions. Marie's sudden death had hit me hard—and not because I'd lost my first and only client. She was just a kid and didn't deserve to go out that way. No one did. I hadn't been able to help Marie when she needed it and that was a burden I'd carry with me for a long time. But it was Kate that I was concerned about now.

Despite assurances that she was fine, she didn't look it. The blood I'd wiped off her face and suit was partly mixed with brain matter and she was still unsteady on her feet. I had to get her away from the scene before the media circus arrived and began to pepper her with a bunch of questions. Fending off their attack would take more strength than either of us possessed now—at least without a stiff drink or two first. We walked a block down Pike Street to Murphy's Pub and grabbed a table at the back of the dark saloon for some privacy.

Murphy's was no fake Irish bar that served green beer on St. Pat's Day to please the Celtic wannabes looking for an excuse to drink themselves into oblivion. Patrick Murphy would've shut the joint down before he'd let that happen. He was a red-haired ex-Dubliner who catered to a rough and rowdy crew of assorted ne'er-do-wells who didn't need a holiday or any other excuse to drink.

The place was packed with true believers when we arrived and smelled of stale beer and working class sweat. The regulars had never given me the time of day when I was still with the department. Now that I was no longer The Man and, in fact, had been unceremoniously kicked out of the ranks, they felt a grudging kinship with me. Murphy had told him that their change in attitude was a lot like life. "We all come into this world buck naked, wet and hungry," he said. "Then things get a whole lot worse. Welcome to Murphy's."

The gang would've greeted me with their usual brand of drunken prattle, but Murphy shut them down right away. He could tell by the set of my jaw that I wasn't in the mood for any of their nonsense. But it didn't stop every Mick in the pub who was still conscious from giving Kate the once-over. She might be a forty-three-year-old grandmother, but Kate Ryan still had the looks that turned heads. Mine included.

As soon as we'd settled at the table and our drinks were on the way, Kate asked, "Why do you think she killed herself?"

"She didn't. Marie was murdered."

"How do you know that?"

"She'd just called me minutes before it happened to tell me she was running late but would meet me shortly. And then she offs herself? By taking a dive from the roof of my own apartment building? No friggin' way."

Murphy arrived with our drinks and set them on the table. "Here ya go, folks. When you're ready for another round, just holler." Kate wasn't much of a drinker, but she snatched the pint of Guinness like it was a life ring and took a big swig. I did the same with Old Bushmills and a beer chaser.

"You might as well get that next round ready now," I told Murphy. He nodded and left us to our misery.

Kate raised an eyebrow but didn't say anything. She didn't have to. I knew she thought I drank too much, whether circumstances justified it or not. It was a major factor in the break-up of our marriage. I've tried hard to get my act together since then but getting canned and starting a new career hasn't exactly been a piece of cake. Kate, though, she's a survivor. She's got the smarts and moxie to get through anything and always has. "How're you doing?" I asked.

"Better," she said. She tucked a strand of hair behind her ear and smiled wanly. I liked that she wore her hair a little longer now. She's a natural redhead but insists it's more strawberry blonde than red. Whatever the color is called, Kate's hair is one of her best features. Her vibrant tresses were what caught my eye when we first met, and all these years later still draws me in. Kate's hair was almost to her waist when we were newlyweds. I used to brush it out for her every night for years. When she opted for a short bob, she said she needed a more updated look. I think she read in some lifestyle magazine that "older" women shouldn't wear their hair past their shoulders. She eyed my shot glass. "How 'bout you? Did the whiskey help?"

I grinned sheepishly. "As always."

"Then tell me about Marie. Why do you think she was murdered?"

"She was being stalked. That's the reason she wanted to hire me. To find out who was stalking her and put a stop to it."

"She didn't know who it was?"

"Not a clue. She just knew she was being followed and it had creeped her out big time."

"Why did you need me to meet with her?"

"It doesn't matter now, does it?"

She frowned as she sipped her drink. "Look," she said. "You insisted that I stop whatever I was doing and hurry downtown to provide your client with some needed expertise. I'd like to know what "expertise" you thought I could possibly contribute to a stalking case."

I was reluctant to tell Kate the truth. Marie Talbot wasn't strictly my client. I'd met with her initially because I'd been referred by a mutual acquaintance. She was scared, but still undecided as to whether she needed to hire me. I tried to put her at ease, and we talked a bit about her studies at the university. She was a so-so engineering student on a scholarship. When she said her grades at summer school were marginal at best, I had an idea. And that's where Kate came into the picture.

"Marie was an engineering student," I said.

"So?"

"So, she was about to lose her scholarship. I thought you might be able to help her out." Kate had been an engineer for most of her working life until her company decided that outsourcing to cheaper foreign labor made more economic sense. But, as I said, she's a survivor. Despite the rotten economy, she landed a new job: concierge at the same complex she helped to build as project engineer. It was a major downgrade in terms of pay and prestige, but Kate made the most of it and thrived.

When things eventually turned sour, she picked herself up again and started over with her own business.

"What do you mean, 'help her out'?"

This is where I knew my explanation would get dicey. I downed the last of my drink and said, "You know, help her with her studies a little."

Kate stared at me like I'd lost my mind, but that was nothing new; I often said things that she found outrageous. "Seriously?" she said. "You actually thought I would be willing to tutor your client?"

What I thought was that Kate would find it difficult to refuse with Marie sitting in front of her. I knew better than to mention that. I shrugged and said, "I just thought if you agreed to help get her grades up, Marie would hire me."

She looked at me incredulously and leaned forward in her chair. "Let me get this straight. Are you telling me Marie Talbot wasn't even your client?"

"Technically speaking, that's correct. But she would've been after our meeting with you."

Kate wasn't impressed with my logic. Nor did she think much of my lame "it seemed like a good idea at the time" grin. She was midway through a not-so-gentle rebuke when Murphy showed up with our second round of drinks. Setting them on the table, he bent over to whisper in my ear. "You got yourself a wee bit of trouble 'bout to head your way." He gestured with his thumb to the front of the saloon.

I usually sit facing the door or window whenever I'm inside a room. It's a cop thing. Old habits die hard, but I'd missed the new arrival until Murphy pointed him out. My former partner stood inside the main entrance and spotted me just as I looked his way. Kevin Gleason made a "pistol" with two fingers and aimed it at me.

"Jesus, have mercy," I said.

Kate whirled around in her seat to see what had made me groan. Gleason's swagger as he crossed the barroom was wasted if he thought anyone at Murphy's—least of all me—would be intimidated. I'd decked him once and wouldn't think twice about doing it again.

"Hello, Kate," he said addressing her with a quick nod. "Nice to see ya'll." Kevin Gleason's drawl was as fake as the southern roots he claimed and about as charming as a prickly cactus. Short and wiry, he exuded a certain Napoleonic bluster that was more disgusting than threatening. What he lacked in height and muscle, he made up for with no-holds-barred ambition. The kind that stomps on anything or anyone who gets in his way.

He didn't wait for Kate to respond before addressing me. "Well, well, well," he said. "If it ain't John Finnegan Doyle. Why am I not surprised to find you here?"

I took a long slow pull on my whiskey. "The question is, why're you here? I thought the yuppie bars in Bellevue were more your style."

"Don't you know? I'm with the Seattle P.D. now."

I managed to hide my surprise. "That a fact?"

"They recruited me," he said proudly. He waited an awkward beat as if expecting me to congratulate him. "I'd let you buy me a celebratory drink but I'm on duty."

"Bummer. Where's your new partner? Quit on you already?"

"Nice try, Doyle. We snagged the Talbot case. She's still at the scene and I volunteered to find you. Didn't take much looking. Just headed to the nearest bar and here you are."

I saluted him with my shot glass. "Ace detective, that's you."

Kate frowned at me, making it clear what she thought of our exchange. Then she looked at Gleason and smiled warmly. "I was an eyewitness to her suicide, not Jack," she said pointing to her blood-stained suit. "Do you need me to make a statement?"

"The Talbot gal didn't kill herself," he said with a condescending smile. "Evidence we found on the roof—the roof of Jack's apartment, no less—points to homicide. It's Jack here who needs to make a statement. He's a person of interest in this case."

A person of interest is cop-speak for: we don't have enough to charge you with yet, so just sit tight while we do some digging until we do. Knowing Gleason, he'd take whatever shortcut he could—which meant he'd already decided I was his number one suspect. "Let me save you some trouble," I said. "I had no reason to want Marie Talbot dead." I glanced at Kate. "She was my first and only client. I needed her."

"That's not what the evidence says."

"What evidence?"

"I don't have to share that with you." He let his pronouncement hang in the air a moment, but it was obvious that he wanted to tell us. He made it sound like he was doing me a favor instead of trying to make me squirm. "You're a civilian now and not entitled to any details. But, as a professional courtesy to a former partner, I will make

16

an exception. The girl put up quite a struggle before she went over. There were scrape marks on the roof like she'd been dragged, and we found one of her sandals and several broken fingernails at the ledge."

"How does that relate to me?" I asked.

"Patience, my man," he said with a raised hand. "I'm getting there. We also found her purse on the roof. There was a signed representation agreement with Arnold DuPont of DuPont Investigations inside. Unless you can produce another agreement dated and signed after she went with DuPont, I'd say your so-called one and only client gave you the royal shaft. Is that why you killed her?"

CHAPTER THREE

KATE

After essentially accusing Jack of murder, Kevin Gleason ordered him to come down to the station the next day for questioning. Jack told him in very graphic terms what he thought of that idea, which brought their testosterone-filled tête á tête to an abrupt ending. It could have been worse. The last time they were together things got physical. Gleason apologized half-heartedly before leaving. "Sorry, Kate," he said. "Maybe you can talk some sense into him. I can't help Jack if he refuses to cooperate."

"Leave her out of this," Jack growled. "We all know what your version of 'help' is, and we aren't interested."

Gleason turned on his heels and stomped out of the saloon. Jack shook his head and said, "What a prick!"

"I don't get it."

"What's to get? It wasn't enough that he ruined my career, now my ex-partner is out to ruin my life, too."

It was true that Gleason pulled some dirty tricks that made him look good at Jack's expense. His maneuvering prevented Jack from earning the credit he deserved for solving a major homicide case and ultimately resulted in his ouster from the BPD. But Jack was already on probation at the time. If he were completely honest, he'd admit that he had a role in his own downfall. Still, he had a point about Gleason. The man did not play nice. "That's not what I'm talking about," I said. "I don't get why you didn't just tell Gleason you had a rock-solid alibi. You were at Java Joe's when Marie was killed."

Jack looked down at the table and ran a finger around his empty glass. "That wouldn't do me any good."

"Why not? The barista and at least some of the customers should be able to verify that you were at the coffee shop."

"I'm sure they would—*if* I'd been there."

"What are you talking about? I saw you along with everyone else who came streaming out of Joe's."

"No, Kate," he said quietly. "You saw me on the sidewalk after she fell. I came out of my apartment building, not Java Joe's."

"Oh." I could just imagine how Kevin Gleason would spin that bit of information. And it wouldn't be to Jack's advantage.

He must have thought he needed to reassure me for he reached across the table and took my hands in his. "Here's the thing, the only thing that's important: I didn't kill Marie."

Jack had his share of faults—enough to ruin two marriages and a good career—but he was no murderer. It saddened me that he felt it necessary to even say so. I squeezed his hand. "You don't need to convince me, Jack. But why weren't you at the coffee shop like we'd arranged?"

"I got delayed," he said with a shrug. "Shit happens."

Jack has a way of avoiding hard truths. There had to be more behind his vague excuse, but it didn't matter right now. I was more concerned with how Gleason's accusations had affected him. His tough guy attitude had disappeared. In its place was a weariness that looked a lot like defeat. His spiffy new suit jacket hung loosely on his slumped shoulders and his eyes, having lost their usual amused sparkle, were glazed again. He ran his hands over his face as if he could wipe away the worry lines wrinkling his brow. He glanced at his empty glass and sighed. When he raised an arm to signal Murphy, I intervened. "Another drink won't help your situation."

He shifted in his chair. "Yeah? What will?"

"A little cooperation. You could go down to the station and talk to Gleason."

"That's a non-starter."

"He'll just take your refusal as proof that you've got something to hide."

"Gleason already thinks that. Don't forget, I worked with the guy. I know how he operates. He'll take whatever I say and twist it to suit his purposes." He shook his head. So, no thanks. I'll pass on cooperation."

"Okay, you've made your point," I said. "That leaves just one other option."

"What's that?"

"Finding Marie's killer. Whoever pushed her off the roof was probably the same person who'd been stalking her. We need to find out who that was."

"*We*?"

"You and me. If I remember correctly, you thought I had a lot to offer the last time we worked on a case together." I never thought I'd hear those words come out of my mouth. Given the way he looked at me, I don't think Jack expected it either.

"Don't go there, Katie. I should never have asked you to be my informant at BellaVilla. I almost got you killed."

"No, I did that all on my own. You'd warned me about not taking unnecessary risks, but I was too stubborn to listen. This time will be different."

"It'll be different all right. You won't be involved in any way, shape or form."

"Look, I'm already involved. Up close and personal. I admit I wanted nothing to do with your client, but that was before she plunged to her brutal death right in front of me. And I never wanted to partner with you again either, but that was before you were accused of killing her—by the same underhanded bully that, for some perverse reason, still has it in for you."

"I thought you had a business to run."

"I do, but it's not like I'm stuck behind a desk all day. I'm out and about a lot—checking in with the various condos I have under contract and meeting with potential new clients. I should have plenty of time available between appointments to follow up on leads for you."

He shook his head vigorously. "No! It's too dangerous. I don't want to put you in harm's way ever again."

"And tutoring a stalking victim wasn't a dangerous situation?"

"I didn't think so at the time. Marie was terrified, but I figured she was just overreacting. A beautiful girl like that attracts a lot of attention. Sometimes the attention gets out of hand. Usually, it's just some misguided jerk who needs a lesson about boundaries. Obviously, I was wrong. It's a murder case now and I don't want you anywhere near it."

Whenever I'd refused to do what Jack wanted in the past, he knew just what to say to change my mind. He was a master at the game, but the student had learned how to play. I decided to ante in. "Yes, it's a murder case," I said. "But, as Gleason so bluntly put it, you're a civilian now, an ex-cop who burned more than a few bridges on the way out the door. And the friends you still have left haven't exactly rallied around you. In fact, you've complained that they haven't been very supportive of your P.I. gig. I bet they'll be even less willing to help when the word gets out about you being a suspect in Marie's murder."

He winced as if I'd slapped him.

"Face it, Jack. You need me now more than ever. You said that you know how Gleason operates. Well, so do I. He's already practically pinned Marie's murder on you. Now all he has to do is make the facts fit his theory. I don't know about you, but I'm not willing to let him get away with that. You've often said that we make a good team. Besides knowing how to deal with people—I am a concierge, after all—I can see the big picture as well as the details. We've had our differences over the years, but we share a daughter and granddaughter together. I'll do whatever it takes to make sure you'll always be in their lives. If that means helping you track down a murderer to prove your innocence, so be it."

He'd listened to my lengthy plea with a stoic expression. When he let a slight smile slip through, I knew I had him. Maybe not at hello, but it was close. He grinned and said, "You've been around me way too much lately. That little speech sounded a lot like the Irish blarney I usually dish out."

"So, we've got a deal?"

"Okay," he said, shrugging. "If you think you can help, I guess it'd be all right. But no unnecessary risks. Are we clear about that?"

"Clear."

The change in his demeanor was immediate. He sat upright in his chair, threw his shoulders back and treated me to a full-out dimpled grin. "That's exactly what I wanted to hear," he said. As he offered me a fist bump to seal the deal, I couldn't help wondering just who'd played whom.

CHAPTER FOUR

JACK

I stayed at Murphy's after Kate left to do whatever successful businesswomen do. Since I had no business, successful or otherwise, I abandoned our table and bellied up to the bar with all the other out-of-work slackers. Murphy brought me the whiskey I'd been about to order when Kate stopped me. It went down smooth and easy. Without a disapproving ex-wife on hand, I didn't feel an ounce of guilt over drinking it or the rest of the rounds that followed. I'd have smoked a few cigarettes if I hadn't kicked the habit about the same time the clean air freaks banned it in public facilities.

"Hey, Murph," I said. "Did you hear the one about the doctor and the drunk?"

He shook his head as he ran a thin damp rag over the countertop. "No," he said, grinning. "What about the doctor and the drunk?"

"Seems the doc tells him that the best thing to do for his health is to give up drinking and smoking, get up early every morning and go to bed early every night. The drunk paused and thought about the advice a moment. Then he asked the doc, "What's the second-best thing to do?""

"I've heard that one before," said the guy on the stool next to me. "And it ain't no joke. My doctor told me the same thing." He laughed as he raised his pint. "You can see how I followed that advice. But hell, I'm still drinkin' and smokin' and my doctor's been in the ground goin' on ten years now."

A few more jokes followed, but I knew that sooner or later someone would bring up Kate. I never talk much about my private life. My downfall with the department was common knowledge, but there are some things I don't care to share—especially with the barroom crowd. They razzed me unmercifully until I finally broke down and told them her name. But that didn't get them off my back. "Come on, man," one of the guys said. "We all want to know how you do it. How does an ugly, no-good loser like you end up with a knock-out like Kate?"

Good question. Kate's offer to help me solve Marie Talbot's murder had been unexpected, but welcome. I'd been sincere when I said I didn't want her exposed to danger. We'd been down that road before. When I was still with the Bellevue Police Department, a couple of the residents in a luxury condominium where Kate worked were murdered. Thanks to her, we solved the case and the killer was caught, but Kate was almost killed in the process. She doesn't blame me, but I still feel guilty about dragging her into the case. Not enough, though, to ban her from ever working with me again.

The truth is, I wasn't nearly as opposed to her involvement as I'd let on. I needed Kate. Always have. The worst mistake of my life was messing up our marriage. My brief second marriage was an even worse disaster and the less said about it the better. Circumstances have thrown Kate and me together again and I'd be stupid to let any chance I might have with her slip away. Our daughter says we belong together, and I agree. Kate can dance around the truth all she wants, but I know she feels the same way about us. She wouldn't be so eager to help me if she didn't.

I shut down further discussion about Kate and killed the rest of the afternoon drinking and chewing the fat. Going home now was out. Running into Kevin Gleason or the rest of the investigation team before the scene had been cleared wasn't my idea of a good time. Tipping back a few at Murphy's seemed like a much more reasonable way to spend an afternoon. Besides, my own investigation into Marie's murder could only be conducted without Gleason and the others around to get in my way.

Once I figured enough time had passed, I hauled my ass off the stool and headed back to my apartment. As I expected, my old partner hadn't forgotten about me. There was a black and white parked at the curb in front of Murphy's when I came outside. I grinned at the cop who'd been ordered to keep tabs on me but didn't engage him further. That I could walk the two blocks to my apartment without stumbling gave me hope that I was still sober. At least sober enough to corner the Trenton Arms' security guard and ask him a few pointed questions.

Tom Lamont was a college kid who worked security part-time while he attended college. He was a geeky sort with eyeglasses thicker than his muscles, but he took his job seriously and was good at keeping the riffraff from wandering into the building. He had a few classes with Marie Talbot and like every other dude over the age of twelve, he'd fallen madly in love with her. I doubt she thought of Tom in the same way but whatever the nature of their relationship, she had confided in him about her stalker. She met with me at his suggestion and never once mentioned that she was also considering the Arnold DuPont agency.

Tom sat at the front desk in the lobby with his nose in a textbook and never noticed me enter the building. Now that the day's drama had ended and the police and looky-loos had departed, the place was back to normal—and quiet enough that Tom could study while on duty. As a rule, the residents don't hang out in the lobby to chitchat with their neighbors. Unlike the trust fund babies and dividend divas Kate deals with, they're mostly working stiffs. Not a poolside-martini-sipping-portfolio-comparing snob in the bunch. They stop by the lobby just long enough to pick up their mail—usually a fistful of bills—before collapsing in front of their TV with a beer. In short, my kind of people. The Trenton Arms didn't have much going for it as far as décor or amenities are concerned, but it was clean and odor-free. The best you could say about the place I called home was that I could afford it. Meaning it was damn cheap.

"Hey, Tom," I said. "Good book?"

When he looked up, his eyes were puffy and rimmed in red. I doubted that the condition was caused by too much reading. He was a sensitive type who seemed ill-suited for security work. I'd seen him cry when my neighbor's dog died. Marie's violent death had to have devastated him. It was somewhat surprising that he was still on duty. It would've been just like him to ditch the rest of his shift after such a trauma. Tom used to work security at Kate's former condo in the burbs but quit without notice when the two residents got murdered. The mean streets of Seattle didn't seem like a safer bet, but he'd lasted here a lot longer than in Bellevue.

"Oh, it's you," he said.

"That's a hell of a greeting, kid."

"Sorry," he said, closing his textbook. "I'm not myself today."

"Understandable. Marie's death was quite a shock."

He shuddered visibly. "It was horrible! I've never seen anything like it. I still can't believe she's dead. Suicide was bad enough, but now they're saying it was murder. Why would anyone want to hurt Marie? She was beautiful but really nice, you know? I mean, she wasn't like some of the girls at school who are too stuck on themselves to even talk to you. Marie was nice to everyone. Even me."

"I hear ya," I said, as Tom wiped fresh tears from his eyes. "Marie Talbot was a special girl."

"That's exactly what I told the cops."

"How'd they treat you?"

"Okay, I guess. It was really strange, though."

"How's that?"

"They asked a million questions about you. I got the impression that they consider you a suspect."

"Aw, that's what homicide dicks do. Target the nearest person around and pin it on him. It's all just for show—a way to look good in the press. When their first choice doesn't pan out, it's on to the next poor sap they can find. You're probably on their radar screen as we speak."

When you've interrogated as many people as I have over the years, you learn what techniques work best. I've found that the faster you can knock someone off-center, the faster they'll tell you what you want to know. Judging from Tom's shocked expression, I'd scored a direct hit.

"M-m-me?" he stuttered. "Why would they think I had anything to do with killing Marie?"

"Did they grill you about seeing her come into the building?"

"Yes, but the detectives told me that was so they could establish a timeline."

"Don't believe anything cops say, kid. I know all the tricks. They wanted to confirm that you were the last person to see her alive."

"But she said she was going to meet with you. At your apartment. Wouldn't that make you the last person to see her?"

"I'm disappointed in you, Tom. You know very well that Marie wasn't my client. She'd already taken your recommendation and hired Arnold DuPont."

"What? I don't know any . . . Arnold? Arnold who?"

"Arnold DuPont. He's one of the most successful—and expensive—private investigators in town. What I want to know is how a college girl on a scholarship could afford his services."

"I didn't—"

"Don't yank my chain, Tom. Just tell me the truth."

"But I *am* telling the truth! I never recommended anyone else to Marie. You're the only P.I. that I know."

"Let's assume for a moment that's true. Why would she say she was meeting me in my apartment? That doesn't make sense. We'd agreed to meet at Java Joe's."

"Right. I knew that. That's why I was surprised to see her here. Marie said the meeting place had been changed at the last minute."

"Did she mention who'd changed the plans?"

"No. I just assumed it was you."

"Never assume anything. You should have checked with me before sending her up on the elevator. That's what security is all about." When he hung his head, I almost felt sorry for the guy, but not enough to suggest that real security would've included some cameras installed at strategic locations throughout the building. Cheap rent has its advantages, but a state-of-the-art security system isn't one of them.

"Let's put the security issue aside for now," I told him, "and get back to Marie. She comes into the lobby. Says she's going to meet with me at my apartment. She gets on the elevator and presumably punches the button for my floor. Then the next thing we know she's flying headfirst off the roof." I paused a moment and eyed him carefully. "A roof that's only accessible through a door that's supposed to be locked 24-7. A door that only you have the key to. How do you explain that?"

I'd rattled his cage earlier, but this line of questioning had him blushing like I'd discovered him watching a porno flick on company time. "I . . . uh . . . uh, the door wasn't locked."

I didn't have to say anything further. Tom Lamont was basically a good guy. And like most good guys who've been caught coloring outside the lines, he felt the need to explain and justify.

"I go up to the roof on my breaks to smoke," he said. "Old Mrs. Snyder complains if I smoke outside the lobby door. I've tried to tell her that I stand well beyond the twenty-five-foot rule, but she still gets on my case. It's just easier to smoke on the roof along with everyone else."

"Everyone else?"

"You know, the residents who smoke. They don't want to deal with Mrs. Snyder any more than I do. It's a toss-up as to which is worse, Mrs. Snyder or the panhandlers. Some of those guys who hang around the building are totally aggressive. And stinky."

"What I hear you saying is that the roof is accessible to anyone at any time."

"I guess so. I gave up trying to keep the door locked. The residents kept propping it open after I'd unlock it for them. That way they could smoke on the roof whenever they wanted without chasing me down for the key." He eyed me nervously. "You won't report me to my boss, will you?"

I rubbed my chin as if thinking the matter over. "Did you tell all this to the detectives who were here?"

"Yes."

"Then your boss already knows. But no worries. Old man Stewart couldn't care less, as long as the residents are happy. And you made them happy. Mrs. Snyder and the smokers, anyway."

Tom exhaled like he'd been holding his breath the whole time. "Thank God."

"You can thank God on your own time. What I want to know right now is why Marie hired Arnold DuPont. And how the hell she could afford the insane fees he charges."

"Maybe you should just ask him."

"No, I'm asking you."

"I have no idea why she hired someone else," he said. Several beats passed before he added, "But maybe Alicia can tell you."

"Who's Alicia?"

"Alicia Gonzales. Marie's roommate."

Tom said they shared an off-campus apartment in Redmond, but he didn't know the address. "You got a phone number for her?" I asked.

"No," he said, glancing at his watch. "But if you hurry, you can catch her at the campus pool. She works out there every day at five o'clock."

CHAPTER FIVE

KATE

I had second thoughts about helping Jack as soon as I left Murphy's. I sort of fudged the truth (okay, lied) when I said I had time to chase down leads for him. It was true that I don't sit behind a desk for eight hours a day anymore, but something always needs my attention—quarterly payroll taxes, candidate interviews, employee uniforms, property management issues, personnel issues, et cetera. Given my jam-packed to-do list, it was probably foolish of me to claim I had time to help Jack. I have a habit of doing foolish things when it comes to my ex. It's a character flaw, but what can I say? To coin an overused phrase, it is what it is.

I could excuse today's offer to partner with him as post-tragedy trauma or the Guinness I'd downed, but it was Kevin Gleason's finger-pointing that closed the deal. The man had it in for Jack. Destroying his career wasn't enough. Gleason wouldn't rest until he'd ruined Jack's life, too. Truth be told, though, Jack was his own worst enemy.

That said, I still had to give him credit. He was struggling, but he hadn't given up—yet. My fear was that Marie's murder and Gleason's threatening accusations would be enough to push him over the edge. He'd already been teetering there ever since he'd left the BPD. A fall now would most certainly lead to a downward spiral from which he couldn't recover. Although he had his faults, Jack has always been a good father and grandfather. I'd hate to see his relationship with Erin and Shannon damaged by a murder charge. My busy schedule aside, I still felt confident that I could help him. I just hoped Jack didn't think it meant my feelings for him had changed. He was still my ex-husband and no matter how sexy I sometimes found him, romance wasn't part of the deal. I wasn't *that* foolish.

The first thing I did after leaving the pub was to call my accountant and cancel our appointment so that I could go shopping. I might've felt confident, but I didn't look it. The restroom mirror at Murphy's told the tale. I needed an overhaul and fast. I did what I could with my make-up and hair, but my blood-splattered suit was beyond fixing. There was no way I could take care of business looking like a walking crime scene. I dashed into Nordstrom's, which was my go-to destination for business attire. Unlike the meeting with my accountant, I'd scheduled some employee interviews for the afternoon in Bellevue that couldn't be postponed without a major hassle.

If I'd known that Nordstrom's was having its half-yearly sale, I would've hiked an extra block to Macy's. I have nothing against saving a few bucks, but crowds tend to make me claustrophobic. I hurriedly elbowed my way through the sales-loving masses and grabbed an outfit that looked decent enough to be seen in ritzy Bellevue. The Ann Taylor number was the last one in my size and the sales price was a bonus. I wanted to change my bloody attire for the new suit in one of the dressing rooms but there were so many other women waiting for an available room that I gave up and headed directly for the cashier's station. I figured I could always change in one of the restroom lounges after I had paid. I'd just joined the end of the lengthy, slow-moving line when I heard someone bellow my name.

"Well, butter my butt and call me a biscuit! If it ain't Kate Ryan!" Because of the hordes of shoppers, I couldn't see the woman who'd hailed me, but I sure recognized her Texas twang and outlandish greeting. Danielle Livingston was a resident at the luxury condo where I'd previously worked. Like her home state, everything about Danielle was big—big hair, big boobs, big attitude, big bank account, but most of all, big heart. She had given me a cover story so that I could help Jack on the last case he worked as a police detective—the case that Kevin Gleason manipulated in order to sandbag Jack's career. Danielle and I didn't exactly run in the same social circles, but we had met for lunch a few times after I left BellaVilla. I'd been so busy starting my business that I hadn't seen her in quite a while. Roaming the aisles of Nordy's petite department was the last place I ever expected to run into her. Danielle was more plus-size than petite and more flash than conservative.

"Good Lord Almighty, girl!" she exclaimed when she caught up with me. "What happened to you?"

I could've said the same thing about her. If it weren't for her familiar voice and biscuit line, I'd hardly have recognized her. Danielle wasn't so big anymore. In fact, I guessed that she was more than a hundred pounds lighter. She looked terrific and I told her so. Since I was getting nowhere fast in the line that was backed up to hell and gone, I avoided explaining my appearance by asking about her remarkable weight loss. "You have to tell me your secret, Danielle."

"Oh, darlin' it was all my dog's fault."

"What?"

"Didn't expect that, did you? The fact is, I dropped a candy bar on the floor and Gizmo got to it before I did. Chocolate wasn't good for either of us, but we both did our best in a desperate tug-a-war to win the treat. I ultimately won and gobbled down the candy as fast as I could. Old Gizmo watched me with what, I swear, was pity on his hairy face. That's when it hit me: wrestling a little dog over a damn candy bar *was* pathetic. Worse than pathetic. I decided then and there to finally get myself in shape. I joined the *Lose to Win* organization that same day." She raised her trim arms in a triumphant gesture. "And Ta-Da . . . the new me is what you see. I'm even a *Lose to Win* Coach now for the Seattle Chapter."

The checkout line slowly inched its way along as I congratulated Danielle on her achievement. "Now, enough about me," she said, eying my damaged suit. "Were you in an accident?"

I fingered one of the stains on my collar. Some of the women in line turned to look at me, apparently eager for an explanation as well. "I guess I was in the wrong place at the wrong time."

"A bloody wrong place, judging from the looks of you."

"A young woman fell off the roof of a building and landed right in front of me." Danielle took the news in stride, but I heard a few gasps around me. "I'm a mess but it could've been a lot worse."

Danielle nodded. "Better a little blood than smashed flat as a pancake. So, did the gal jump or get pushed off the roof?"

"The police think it's murder."

Danielle is tough as nails and twice as smart. "How do you know that? Don't tell me your good-lookin' Irish charmer is on the case. I thought Jack worked in Bellevue."

"Not exactly." I didn't want to get into Jack's fall from grace. "Jack's a private investigator in Seattle now and the woman was his first paying client. So, he has a vested interest in the case." No need to mention that he's also Gleason's prime suspect.

Her once chubby face broke into a sly grin. "Has he roped you into helping him again?" Danielle was convinced that Jack was still in love with me and that's why he was always inventing some excuse to be around me.

I sighed. "It's complicated."

"Uh-huh," she said skeptically. "When are you going to admit that you haven't gotten over him yet? You know he loves you truly, madly, deeply, and all that."

"Oh, Danielle, please. We're divorced and that's the way it's going to stay."

She chuckled. "Whatever you say, sugah, but methinks the lady doth protest too much." When Texas twang meets Shakespeare quotes, I knew Danielle wasn't finished with my love life or the lack thereof. Luckily, I was saved when the cashier yelled, "Next!"

"Sorry, but that's me," I said. "I've got to go."

"Sure thing. But let's get together soon. I'd like to get your take on a new business idea I have."

"Sounds good. I'll give you a call. You're still at BellaVilla, right?"

Danielle hooted. "Hell, no! That place ain't the same without you running the show. I'm living in Seattle now. Call me on my cell phone. It hasn't changed."

****

I made it to the Westin Hotel in my new suit with enough time to grab a coffee at the Starbucks next door. The Westin is one of the newer hotels in Bellevue. It has a minimalist décor with clean lines and an upscale, sophisticated appearance that the wealthy Seattle suburb is known for. I conducted my candidate interviews at the hotel because the lobby is similar to The Millennium, a new condo whose management just signed a contract with me. The condo catered to young, hip professionals who weren't shy about flaunting their wealth and status. I figured if the candidates felt at ease among the hotel's well-heeled clientele, they'd do fine at the Millennium. I'd lined up six interviews back to back, although I'd received twice that many resumés for the one concierge position that I'd advertised.

I'd just settled into a chair and taken a sip of my latte when my first interviewee arrived. Laura Latimore was on the downhill side of fifty and looked it. As Danielle would say, "she'd been rode hard and put up wet." The photo (unrequested by me) she'd attached to her resume was outdated by at least twenty years. Not that I have anything against older workers. If anything, I'm partial to anyone who has reached "a certain age" since I fit into that category myself. And, I've found that the older worker usually has a strong work ethic. Punctuality, dependability, and excellent customer service skills, not age, were at the top of my hiring needs list. I looked at my watch. Ms. Latimore was punctual, so she was off to a good start. She took a moment to survey the lobby before focusing on me.

As she approached, I stood and greeted her. "Laura? I'm Kate Ryan."

CHAPTER SIX

JACK

The University of Washington's main campus—U-Dub as the locals call it—is situated on 703 acres of prime real estate in the University District of downtown Seattle. Founded in 1861 to encourage economic development in the city, it has more than fulfilled that goal over the decades. Seattle currently has a booming economy and is one of the fastest growing cities in the United States, so say the boosters at the Chamber of Commerce.

Kate earned her degree in engineering from the U-Dub with magna cum laude honors. Our daughter Erin graduated summa cum laude in computer science. Two sharp cookies. Me? Not so much. I attended a local community college and majored in police science and criminal justice. The certifications were not as prestigious as a degree from the University of Washington, but it was enough to get me into the police academy to start my career.

Tom said I could find Marie's roommate, Alicia Gonzales, at the Pavilion Pool on campus. She'd injured her leg in a motorcycle crash and swam at the pool every day for therapy. I arrived just as students began to stream out of the building, along with a strong waft of chlorine. Lean and athletic looking, every one of them could pass for an Olympic competitor. The exception was Alicia Gonzales. She lagged behind the other students and walked with a severe limp that slowed her progress toward a nearby bicycle rack. No motorcycle in sight.

Tom had told me about her limp, but it was minor, compared to her overall appearance. She was short and chubby with a fierce scowl plastered on her round face that looked like a permanent feature. Add in the numerous piercings on her lips, eyebrows and God only knows where else, she exuded a "don't mess with me" vibe. But in case you missed it, her white sleeveless tank top reinforced the tough girl look with bold red letters saying, *Wanna Get Bitch Slapped?* She wore the tank top over too-tight cut-off denim shorts frayed at the ends. Her hair was shaved except for a purple dyed mullet tied in a mini ponytail atop the center of her head. Tattoos covered her arms from both shoulders to both wrists. I'd seen biker gangs in Seattle that looked less intimidating than Alicia Gonzales. The heavy-duty backpack slung over her shoulder probably held an AR47 instead of books. And she roomed with Marie Talbot? No way, no how.

"Alicia? Alicia Gonzales?" She had made it to the bicycle rack by the time I approached her. She didn't look at me until she'd unlocked her bike chain and stuffed it into her backpack.

"Who wants to know?" she demanded. Her dark penetrating eyes signaled that she better like my answer. She didn't.

"I'm Jack Doyle," I said, projecting what I hoped was a friendly, non-threatening look.

"I don't talk to fuckin' cops," she said, dismissing and insulting me in one fell swoop.

"I'm not a cop, but they will be contacting you soon. Marie Talbot was murdered today."

"Bullshit."

"I'm sorry, but it is true. Since you're her roommate, they will want to talk to you about her death."

She didn't seem convinced. "And just how do you know so much about Marie and her so-called murder?" she asked skeptically.

I fished out my P.I. license from my wallet and held it so she could see it. "Marie hired me to find out who was stalking her."

"Ha! Some P.I you are," she scoffed. "A murder on your watch. Bravo! If it happened at all, it wouldn't have been a stalker. Marie wasn't stalked by anyone or she would've told me."

"Maybe she didn't want to worry you."

"Do I look like the worrying kind, Mr. P.I. man?"

She had me there. Alicia's look was more apt to give others cause to worry. "Maybe not, but surely you must have known something was bothering Marie. She seemed really nervous and upset when she met with me."

"Look, I don't know what your game is, but I have nothing to say about Marie," she said, climbing onto her bike.

Before she took off, I tossed one of the cards that I'd designed and printed myself at Kinko's into her bike's front basket. "In case you change your mind, my number is on the card. Call me anytime."

She gave me the middle finger salute as she pedaled away.

"That went well," said a voice behind me.

I turned around to face one of the student swimmers I'd seen coming out of the Pavilion pool earlier. He was a hottie as my daughter would say. I wouldn't go that far, but he did have all the requisite tall, dark and handsome good looks that women seem to go for. Handsome or not, I didn't appreciate his sarcasm. "It's a start," I said lamely.

"Is it true that Marie was murdered?" he asked with a concerned frown.

"Yes. It happened just this morning. Did you know her?"

"The whole engineering department knew Marie Talbot. I had several classes with her, and we were in a study group together. She was a brilliant student and well-liked, too. Why would anyone want to harm, let alone, kill Marie?"

"That's what I'm trying to find out." I could believe that Marie was well-liked but a brilliant student? According to her, she was about to lose her scholarship. Unlike Alicia Gonzales, he seemed willing to talk. I held out my hand. "My name's Jack Doyle," I said as we shook. "You probably heard me tell Alicia that I'm a P.I. Do you have some time to get a cup of coffee?" I asked. "I'd like to ask you a few questions that may help me find her killer."

He had a firm handshake. "I'm Scott Patterson," he said. "I'm done with classes for the day, but my part-time job at the HUB starts soon." He consulted the Fitbit on his wrist. "I can probably spare fifteen minutes or so, but I really don't know what I can tell you that would help much."

"Let me be the judge of that," I said.

Since Scott worked at the student union building—also known as the HUB—he suggested we talk there so he would have a little more time before his shift started.

The line was long at the coffee bar, but Scott flashed his employee badge and got us served right away. I think the cute barista would've gladly served Scott first even without his badge. Her flirty smile and playful wink were over-the-top obvious. I didn't get so much as a brief nod in my direction. I'd have liked an Irish coffee but settled for a latté. Scott said he was in training and avoided caffeinated drinks. He ordered a lemonade.

We settled at a table that afforded us some privacy for our discussion. Mindful of the limited time Scott had available, I started questioning him right away. "How well did you know Marie?" I asked.

"I guess as well as anyone she dated," he said after he'd swallowed a sip of his drink.

"How long did you date Marie?"

"Just a couple of times is all. Studying and swim team practice takes up a lot of my time."

"Then Marie wasn't your girlfriend?"

He shook his head sadly. "No, but I would've liked her to be."

"But?"

"Marie was really popular on campus. And not just because of her looks. She had a great personality and was a lot of fun to be around. She was friends with everybody, including the girls. I was just one of the many guys she dated."

"So, no steady boyfriend?"

"She did last year. The guy was a freshman then, too, and they'd dated all through high school in their hometown."

"Why'd they break up?"

"I'm not sure, but I suspect it was because of all the attention Marie got from so many other men."

"What's this ex-boyfriend's name?"

Scott's dark eyes grew wider. "You don't think he could've had something to do with her murder, do you?"

"A jilted lover is always a suspect."

"I don't know if he was jilted or they just grew apart. College is a lot different from high school and change is inevitable."

"Yeah, I can understand that, but I would like to talk to her former flame anyway. Maybe he knows something that could steer me in the right direction."

"Okay, I guess that makes sense. His name is Rod Dutton and he's in the Delta Chi fraternity."

Scott downed the last of his lemonade and headed to work while I dumped my half-full latté in the trash and Googled the location of the Delta Chi frat house.

CHAPTER SEVEN

KATE

Interviewing potential employees is my least favorite responsibility. Someone can look like the ideal candidate on paper and turn out to be the absolute worst possible candidate in person. While some disastrous performances (and an employment interview is the very definition of performance art) can be attributed to a bad case of nerves or lack of self-confidence, some performances are unusual and, in rare cases, downright bizarre. I once had a candidate take off her shoes during an interview and rub her aching feet (which stunk), another interviewee took a call on his cell phone, explaining that it was a very important job lead, but the most unsettling experience was when an otherwise acceptable candidate said she was very thirsty and asked if she could have a drink of my iced tea. When I refused and offered her bottled water instead, she asked indignantly, "Why not? Do you think I have cooties or something?" She didn't make the cut, cooties or not. The three mistakes I see candidates do most often during an interview are: texting or checking social media on their cell phone, dressing inappropriately, and talking negatively about current or previous employers. Deal breakers, all.

For the most part, my interviews this afternoon went well. Despite her weary, downtrodden appearance, Laura Latimore was dressed professionally and came across as articulate and intelligent. She answered my questions thoughtfully and asked pertinent questions about the duties of the job. We hit it off immediately. I think it was because we had so much in common. She'd held a responsible career in I.T. for over twenty years until her employer decided that outsourcing was the way to go. Not only was her job eliminated, but she had to train her foreign replacement if she wanted a severance package. My former engineering job was similarly outsourced during the economic downturn and I slogged through a ton of interviews without success until I lowered my expectations and accepted the only job I could get— concierge at the very same building for which I'd previously been the project engineer. I suspect that was only because the hiring official once dated my daughter and knew me. Although technically oriented, Laura had excellent communication skills and a willingness to work hard. Her computer expertise was a plus.

Two other candidates didn't fair so favorably. Brittany was an attractive, outgoing blonde in her twenties. I asked the standard "what are your major strengths?" question and she responded that she was punctual. When I reminded her that she had arrived for the interview fifteen minutes late, she called me a "nitpicker." Rodney was in his mid-forties with bloodshot eyes and suffering from what appeared to be a bad hangover. I asked him where he saw himself in five years and he replied, "In the cemetery. My liver's shot." I had to give him points for honesty, but he was a no-go like Brittany. At the end of the day, three out of the six candidates I'd interviewed made it to the top of my hiring list. I wanted to think about all of them overnight, but I was leaning toward selecting Laura Latimore.

I'd turned my cell phone off during the interviews and when I turned it back on, I saw that I'd missed three calls from Danielle Livingston. She sounded upset in the voice mail messages she'd left and insistent that I return her call as soon as possible. I couldn't imagine what had happened to distress someone as unflappable as Danielle. She answered my call on the first ring.

"Oh, thank God," she said. "I've been trying to reach you all afternoon."

"I had my phone turned off and—"

She started sobbing before I could continue. Now I was alarmed. I'd never known Danielle to get even teary-eyed, let alone cry so hard that she sobbed. Danielle," I said. "What's happened?" When she didn't respond, I shouted, "Danielle! Talk to me! What's going on?"

After a moment, she stopped her tearful outburst long enough to gasp, "I can't believe this. It's just unreal."

"Please, Danielle," I said in what I hoped was a caring and comforting voice, "tell me what has upset you. I want to help if I can." She'd called me so she must have thought I could help in some way. As concierge, I often functioned as a sympathetic ear when residents were distressed. Sometimes I felt like I manned a confessional instead of a concierge desk. The stories I heard were . . . well, let's just say I could write a book.

"That gal you told me about? The one who got pushed off the roof?"

"Yes, Marie Talbot."

"No, no. Her name was Marija Trstenjak."

"What? That can't be right. She told Jack her name was Marie. Who is Marija?"

"She was my niece," Danielle groaned.

I was confused. "Wait a minute," I said. "Why do you think the murdered woman is your niece?"

"Because my ex-husband called and told me. The police had notified his sister, Marija's mother, in Yakima, about her death. It was just like you described earlier today. She was pushed off a roof in Seattle."

"Oh, my, God! I'm so sorry, Danielle." What were the chances that two young women had died in the same way on the same day in the same city? Had Marie given Jack a fake name? And, if so, why?

"Do you think you could come over to my place? I really need to talk to someone."

"Of course. Just give me your address and I'll be there right away."

Right away was absurdly optimistic given it was commute time. "The Eastside" is what locals call Bellevue and a mix of other smaller cities and towns that stretch from Lake Washington eastward into the foothills of the Cascades. The area has experienced an explosive growth rate in the last several years, resulting in a huge increase in traffic with longer and longer commute times. The Eastside and Seattle are connected by two floating bridges spanning

Lake Washington. I chose the I-90 bridge rather than the redesigned SR-520 toll bridge, which turned out to be a mistake. Besides the usual stop-and-go traffic, a major accident involving three cars caused a lengthy delay. It was only nine miles from Bellevue to Seattle, but it might as well have been ninety. I arrived at Danielle's Seattle condo an hour and a half after our phone conversation.

Danielle lived at One Plaza, an older building that had been recently renovated from a so-so apartment complex to an upscale condominium. The look and feel of the new renovations were (in my opinion) over-the-top in the glitz and glamour department but seemed to please the well-off crowd. Many of the units were sold in advance and by the time renovations had been completed, the rest were gone in a matter of weeks. The place had all the standard amenities you'd expect in a luxurious residential building that catered to the wealthy. It even had a uniformed doorman, which was a unique feature for condos in Bellevue and Seattle. Unlike New York where doormen are commonplace, it's the concierge who is responsible for greeting and admitting visitors. I'd toured the building before it opened in hopes of securing a contract for Premier Concierge Services, but management selected another firm. I wish I'd known Danielle had bought one of the units. I'm confident she would've put in a good word for me.

Danielle lived on the 32nd floor and had a fantastic view of the city and Lake Union. But I hadn't come to enjoy the view. The delay in my arrival had given Danielle time to pull herself together a bit. Her eyes were red and puffy, but she wasn't crying any more. She invited me into the living room after we embraced, and I offered my condolences. We sat facing each other in burgundy leather chairs separated by a glass coffee table. Her furnishings weren't glitzy like the lobby downstairs but much better in terms of taste. The décor suited Danielle's personality—comfy and welcoming.

"I'm so glad you got here finally," she said. "I'd 'bout given up."

"Traffic was a killer today." I realized my poor choice of words when she winced. "Sorry, that was insensitive of me."

She accepted my apology with a shrug. "That's all right, kiddo. I've got to come to grips with the fact that Mariji was killed. Such a waste." She pointed to the wet bar across the spacious room. "You want a drink? She gestured to her partially filled glass on the coffee table and added unnecessarily, "I've already opened the Scotch."

The Guinness I'd had with Jack was enough for one day. I declined the Scotch but told her to go ahead if she wanted a refill. I felt exhausted by the day's events and drinking alcohol now would put me to sleep. I still had to drive back to Bellevue.

"Are you sure? It's single malt Glenlivet. I brought back a case when I was in Scotland last spring." Ever since she discovered on Ancestry.com that her ancestors hailed from Scotland and Ireland she has traveled to the British Isles a lot, mostly to tour as many whiskey distilleries as possible. When Jack heard about her travels, he joked that she could take him along on the whiskey tours anytime she wanted. Danielle was fond of Jack but assured me that would never happen. "Being with Jack on a distillery tour," she said, "would make me as nervous as a long-tailed cat in a room full of rocking chairs."

"Tell me about your niece," I prompted as she refilled her glass.

"Niece by marriage to my third husband, Billy Bob Cameron. Marija is the daughter of his sister Sally Ann. Marija was a delightful child, and even though I divorced her uncle I stayed in touch with her as she grew up." Danielle shook her head sadly. "I'm going to really miss her," she said in a trembling voice.

I waited while she took a sip of her Scotch and then asked, "What about the rest of Marie's . . . uh, Marija's family? Do you keep up with them as well?"

Danielle scowled, "Not hardly! Sally Ann is beautiful but cold and distant. Marija got her good looks from her but that was about all the woman ever gave her daughter. I always got the impression that motherhood was a burden she never wanted and resented Marija for thrusting her into the role. Her stepfather, Dirk Trstenjak, is even worse. He's tougher than a two-dollar steak and so stupid he'd kick a cow chip on a hot day. As we say back home, Dirk is 'all foam and no beer.' He never adopted Marija but insisted she call herself a Trstenjak after he and Sally Ann were married. Sally Ann was a single mother of one-year-old Marija by a previous relationship and Dirk was divorced with a three-year-old son, Dirk Junior. Junior was an ornery little hellion as a kid and, according to Marija, not much has changed since then. It's an understatement to say Marie had a difficult home life. I was glad when she got her scholarship to the university and could escape her troubled family." Danielle downed the last of her glass and filled it again.

"When did you last see your niece?" I asked.

"We had lunch together just last week. I met her at a café in University Village."

"How did she seem?"

"Happy. Bubbly, even. It was such a delight to be around that gal."

"So, she didn't mention being afraid or nervous lately, like something was bothering her?"

"Not at all. She seemed a little concerned about her studies, but she tends—or I guess I should say tended— to be a perfectionist and pushed herself dang hard. It's paid off since she was a straight 4.0 student." Danielle smiled for the first time. "You would've liked her, Kate. She was going to be an engineer, too."

We talked a bit more, but Danielle said nothing about her niece that even hinted at stalking or safety concerns in any way. Was Marie just putting on a happy face for her aunt? Or, was something else going on? Jack's description of Marie's troubles with her studies and her frightened demeanor didn't jibe with what Danielle had said. I called Jack on my mobile as I drove home. I got his voice mail and left a message. "Jack, we need to talk. I have some new information about Marie that you need to hear." He called me back just as I was parking at my apartment complex. He wanted to come over right away, but I quickly shot down that idea. I needed to take a hot shower and climb into bed as soon as possible. "Then meet me for breakfast," he said. "I have some info to share with you, too."

CHAPTER EIGHT

JACK

Mama's Place is a hole-in-the-wall café on a major street in the University District that everyone calls The Ave. An old-timer once told me that the Ave got its nickname in 1919, when the street was officially known as 14th Avenue NE. Locals apparently felt a numbered street was not a suitable name for the principal business street in the University District. Go figure. The street was ultimately renamed and has been known as The Ave ever since.

I chose to meet Kate at Mama's for sentimental reasons. Kate claims that she doesn't have a sentimental bone in her body, but that's the engineer in Kate talking. The Irish in Kate tears up whenever she hears songs like *Danny Boy* or *The Last Rose of Summer.* Her tears flow at sappy chick flicks, romance novels, and Hallmark cards. Yes, Kate's sentimental all right and I play on that trait whenever I can. In Mama's case, I'd hoped that the café reminded her of all the breakfasts we used to have there back in the day. We were young and in love and would've eaten breakfast, lunch, and dinner together if our college schedules had allowed it. But it was breakfast at Mama's that we most often managed to arrange. I'm not a go-to-church-every-Sunday man, but I do believe in the power of prayer. I've made sure the good Lord knows how my heart feels about Kate.

I arrived at the café early to get us a good table. The place is so small and so popular that if you want to avoid settling for an order to go, you get to Mama's early. The food, not the décor or room size, is the reason for the eatery's popularity.

"Really, Jack? Mama's?" Kate said as she sat down at the table.

Didn't I say she was a smart cookie? I shrugged at her comment as if I had no idea what choosing Mama's Place implied. "Can't go wrong with the food here," I said, smiling innocently.

"Right," she sighed. She turned to look at the plethora of Husky memorabilia that decorated the newly painted walls. "The place has been spruced up a bit since we used to hang out here."

"New owners and new décor but the same great menu," I said, sliding the laminated single sheet of paper in her direction. "I already know what I want."

"Don't tell me," she chuckled. "Biscuits and country gravy with bacon on the side?"

I grinned. "Yep. And I suppose you're going to have your usual toast, scrambled eggs and hash browns?"

"Actually, I follow a plant-based diet now. Don't see much to choose from here," she said, quickly scanning the menu.

"Plant-based? Don't tell me you've become a vegetarian."

"No, I just try to eat mostly fruits, vegetables, fish and whole grains while limiting unhealthy fats."

I didn't want to get into a lecture on healthy eating, so I signaled the server that we were ready to order. Kate found a fruit cup and whole wheat toast to her liking while I stuck with the fatty stuff.

Because there were too few tables for too many people waiting impatiently in line to eat, we couldn't linger over breakfast if we valued our lives. Kate said she had a meeting with her accountant afterward, so our time together would've been short even at a larger diner. "You said last night that you had something to tell me. What did you find out?" I asked, between bites.

"Do you remember Danielle, one of the residents who lived at BellaVilla when I was the concierge there?"

"Who could forget that larger-than-life character? I assume you're referring to the Texan divorcée who married a string of rich oil men and wound up richer than all of them combined."

"Yes, that's Danielle," she said. "I happened to run into her at Nordstrom's. Turns out, Marie Talbot is her niece by marriage to one of her exes."

"Whoa! Didn't see that coming. What did she say about her?"

"She didn't know about Marie's death at the time I saw her, but she called me later crying, and very distraught. She asked me to come over to her condo in Bellevue, which I did. According to Danielle, Marie Talbot isn't her real name. It's Marija Trstenjak."

"Trstenjak? Are you sure we're talking about the same young woman?"

"I'm sure. Danielle's ex called to tell her that Marija had been killed. What are the chances that two different women would fall to their deaths from the roof of the same building on the same day?"

"But why would she lie about her name?"

"Danielle said there were some family issues and Marija changed her name as soon as she turned eighteen."

"What family issues?"

"She's never gotten along with her stepfather, Dirk Trstenjak," Kate said. "But that's not all. Danielle said she wasn't in any danger of losing her scholarship. In fact, she was a 4.0 student. And she didn't seem nervous or upset about anything when Danielle met with her at lunch recently."

I was stunned by Marie's curious subterfuge. She was either an accomplished liar or a damn good actress. I'd been totally convinced that she needed my help. "So," I said, shaking my head, "she was going by a different name, had no academic problems, and maybe didn't even have a stalker after her. Why spin such a tall tale when she met with me?"

"And why did she contact you at all, especially after she'd already hired that other P.I.?"

"Arnold Dupont. The most expensive P.I. in Seattle."

"That's another thing. How does a college student on a scholarship afford him? Danielle said the Trstenjak family isn't rich or even well off. Her stepfather is something of a loser and they are barely getting by. Danielle's ex-husband is the brother of Marija's mother and has offered to help out financially from time to time, but Dirk has rejected all offers."

"Had Danielle been giving her money?"

"I never asked her, but I doubt it. I'll talk to her again to make sure."

"Okay, sounds good. If you have time, there is someone else I'd like you to talk with."

"Who's that?"

"A real jewel by the name of Alicia Gonzales. I met her on campus, but our so-called conversation was a non-starter. She's supposedly Marie's roommate but I sure can't picture them living together. She's nothing like Marie and gave me the royal brush-off PDQ.

"What? You mean your famous Jack Doyle charm failed to impress her?" Kate teased, smiling.

"She made it clear that she didn't talk to cops or private investigators and refused to believe that Marie had even been murdered."

"Why do you think she'd talk to me? And don't tell me it's because I'm not a cop or P.I."

I paused to chew the last of the gravy-drenched bacon that was left on my plate. Kate had finished her so-called plant-based breakfast long before me. "No, but you do ride a motorcycle," I said.

"*Used* to ride a motorcycle," Kate countered.

"That's why you're the perfect person to get her to open up. Alicia was injured in a motorcycle crash and walks with a severe limp now."

"Oh, Jack, please. Just because I rode a bike years ago and had a bad accident also doesn't mean we'll hit it off."

I shrugged. "Maybe not, but it's worth a try. We need to get a better understanding of who Marie or Mariji really was and her roommate is a potentially good source of information. I learned from another student yesterday that Marie had a steady boyfriend but broke up with him to date others. I'm going to track him down and get a read on whether he's a viable suspect. Maybe Alicia can give you some insight into his relationship with Marie. You did promise to help me," I added with a pleading puppy eyes look.

Kate shrugged. "Okay, okay. But you don't have to remind me that I'd promised to help you or make up reasons for me to talk to people. I am willing to help, Jack. Just don't try to manipulate me."

"Fair enough," I said.

"Where does Alicia live?"

"Tom, the guard at my apartment building, told me Alicia and Marie lived in an apartment in Redmond."

Kate's eyebrows shot up. "I know housing is scarce around the university, but Redmond seems like quite a commute traffic-wise."

"I thought so too, but there is a direct bus route. Alicia rides a bicycle now and the bus would easily accommodate it. Who knows, maybe they car-pooled so that they could use the faster HOV lane." I handed Kate a Post-It note. "Anyway, here's the address I found for them."

Once we'd paid our tab and left, we briefly paused outside so I could thank Kate again for her help. She even let me hug her. Mission accomplished.

CHAPTER NINE

KATE

I felt uneasy after my breakfast meeting with Jack. Not because he chose Mama's Place to eat. If he was trying to be subtle about his intentions, he missed the mark. I know that he thinks we'll somehow recapture what we once had if we can just cruise down memory lane often enough. This wasn't the first time he'd arranged a setting for sentimental purposes, so I wasn't surprised. I suppose it was kind of sweet in a way but he's delusional if he thinks I'd fall for him again. No, Jack just being Jack isn't the problem. What bothered me about our meeting was what I failed to bring up: why wasn't he at Java Joe's? One thing you can always count on with Jack is his punctuality. With a meeting as important as signing his first client, he would've been at Java Joe's early. Where was he when Marie fell off the roof of his apartment building? Why was she even at his building? When I'd asked him yesterday about the nature of his delay, he brushed it off as seemingly unimportant. Maybe that was true, but I feared Jack was hiding something he didn't want me to know. Something damaging.

After I left Mama's I fed the parking meter I'd found earlier and decided to walk the three blocks to my accountant's office building. It was a pleasant day and Seattleites know it's best to take advantage of good weather when we can. Especially since the forecast was for intermittent rain showers arriving later in the day. I would have enjoyed my walk more if I hadn't had to dodge the aggressive panhandlers who lined the sidewalks vying for passersby's "donations." Seattle, like many large cities in the country, has a homeless problem that seems to be getting worse as time goes on.

As if to prove my point, a scruffy bearded guy in dirty jeans and ragged shirt lay on the sidewalk with his arms and legs outstretched at an odd angle. At first glance I thought he was injured and needed help, but when I got closer, I could hear him snoring loudly. A black Labrador tied to an over-flowing shopping cart stood alongside his sleeping owner. A cardboard sign hung around the dog's neck with crude lettering that said, *"Please help us. Anything will do. God Bless."* I don't usually contribute to panhandlers, but I'm a sucker when it comes to dogs. Using a dog to elicit sympathy for a donation was an obvious but good tactic. The Lab looked so skinny and hungry that I dropped a few dollars in the bucket next to him. I hoped the guy would at least feed his dog, if not himself, with some of the money.

I felt lucky to have Richard Wycoff as my accountant. He's well known in Seattle and has a lengthy client list for his CPA and CFP services. As soon as I knew I would be starting Premier Concierge I contacted Richard to set up an LLC for my business. I'd known him in college, although we hadn't kept in touch since graduation. But he seemed glad to hear from me and agreed to take me on as a client despite a waiting list. Another case of it's who you know that opens doors. We weren't in the same departments— he was business administration and I was engineering-- but we were both on the golfing teams at U-Dub. The men's and women's teams often had social functions together and I'd met Richard at a party. He was captain of the men's team and I was captain of the women's team. We just sort of naturally gravitated towards one another. We even dated a couple of times, but when Jack entered my life Richard Wycoff had no chance for a third date. As it turned out, I'd made a young and foolish mistake. That's not to say Jack and I didn't have a good marriage for most of the twenty years we were together. The best part of our relationship was the birth of our daughter Erin. She more than makes up for the problems between Jack and me. Like a lot of kids, she still thinks her father and I belong together. Jack and Erin are on the same page in that regard, but I'm not even in the same book.

Richard comes from a very wealthy family. His ancestors were some of the first settlers in the area and were contemporaries of the Denny, Mercer, and Boren families who are credited with founding Seattle. The Wycoff building where Richard has his office sits on property that was the Wycoff's original homestead. Most of the businesses in the building are financial in nature. I took the express elevator which sped me directly to the

35th floor. The Richard Wycoff Company, Inc. occupied the entire floor. I entered the reception area—a large, ultra-modern space with original artwork on the walls. I'm not an art connoisseur but even I recognized the more famous Masters' works on display, including two of Pablo Picasso's paintings. Molly, the attractive receptionist on duty, wore the same suit I'd fallen in love with at Neiman Marcus, but had to pass on. The four-hundred-seventy-five-dollar price tag was more than my budget allowed. Richard must pay his receptionist well or she budgets better than I do. She acknowledged me in a warm and friendly manner, as usual, and escorted me immediately to Richard's office.

Richard rose from a plush leather executive chair to greet me. He'd been sitting behind a sparkling clean glass-topped desk that contrasted sharply with the clutter of folders and paperwork atop a nearby worktable. "Kate, how are you doing?" he asked, clasping my hand in his. "So glad you could make it today."

He didn't sound irritated that I'd messed up his tight schedule, but I felt bad about the inconvenience my cancellation yesterday had no doubt caused. "I'm so sorry, Richard. I know how busy you are and apologize for having to reschedule."

"Nonsense," he said. "I understand completely. The traumatic incident you witnessed yesterday would unnerve anyone."

"It was bad, but I'm grateful that you were able to slip me into your schedule today."

"Not a problem at all." He gestured to a set of golf clubs in the corner of the lavishly furnished room. "Friday is golf day, so no clients were scheduled."

I'd noticed that he wasn't dressed in one of his usual Saville Row custom suits when I'd first entered the office, but it hadn't registered that his collared, short-sleeved polo shirt and casual looking trousers were golfing attire. I just assumed that his office observed a Casual Friday dress code. The receptionist's suit should have been a clue that that wasn't the case. "Oh no," I said. "I've interrupted your day off."

"Hey, it's okay. Our meeting shouldn't take that long." He paused and then grinned. "Perhaps you could join me on the links. For old time's sake."

I was flattered by the invitation but rather taken aback. Did he feel sorry for me? I glanced out the floor-to-ceiling windows a moment to consider my response.

The view of downtown Seattle was breathtaking. So was Richard. In his mid-forties, he was still as good-looking as when we were in college. His hair was just as thick and wavy, without even a hint of gray. He hadn't let his athletic body slide a bit over the years, either, and looked just like the college jock he once was. The only wrinkles he had were laugh lines at the edges of his dark brown eyes. In short, he was a gorgeous hunk of maleness.

I decided that he was just being kind to an old friend who'd been through a horrible experience and I appreciated his thoughtfulness. "I'd like to go golfing again," I said, but I can't take the day off. I have a ton of work to do before I can even think about golfing any time soon."

"Well," he sighed, "maybe you'd have time for a drink at the end of your busy day. I'd meet you anywhere that's convenient for you."

I'd heard that he was single again after losing his wife to a brain tumor a few years ago. With his good looks, fortune, and social prominence he was considered quite a catch. But his unexpected invitation left me fumbling for an answer. I have a strict policy about not combining work and play. Not that I wouldn't have liked to have gone out with Richard. What woman wouldn't? He was fun to be around, and I enjoyed his company a lot, but I had to regretfully decline. "No, Richard. I try to keep my professional associations separate from my social life."

He chuckled. "Hell, Kate, that's why golf was invented. I can't begin to list all the clients I've done business with over a round of golf. The sport and the 19th hole afterward are very good for business. You should consider it."

"I don't doubt what you're saying but mixing golf and clients won't work for me. Thank you for the invitation, though."

"Anytime you change your mind let me know. That drink invitation still stands, too."

We conducted the rest of our meeting without further discussion of golf or our social lives and I was soon on my way home.

I'd just exchanged my suit and blouse for jeans and a short-sleeved shirt when the doorbell rang. I wasn't expecting anyone and had dressed casually for what I hoped would be a successful meeting with Alicia Gonzales. I hadn't called to let her know that I planned to visit. If she were as standoffish as Jack claimed, I thought a more relaxed look would go over better than a power suit.

When I opened the front door, I couldn't believe who was standing on my doorstep. "Kevin Gleason, what are you doing here?"

"Conducting a homicide investigation," he smirked. "And you're a witness I need to talk to."

"I can't help you with your investigation," I said. "All I saw was the aftermath and you didn't seem interested in what I had to say before."

"Nevertheless, I have some questions for you now. May I come in?"

"This isn't a good time. I was just about to go out," I said, starting to close the door.

Gleason blocked the door with his foot like a pesky salesman who wouldn't take no for an answer. "It's important that I talk to you, Kate. Why don't you come down to the station tomorrow?"

That's the last thing I wanted to do. "Sorry, I have meetings all day tomorrow. I run my own business now and it keeps me very busy."

"Hmmf," he snorted. "Be that as it may, if you don't cooperate with my investigation, I can get a warrant for your appearance as a material witness."

"I thought material witness warrants were only issued when a suspect was in custody. Do you have someone in custody?"

"Not yet," he admitted. "But you know our prime suspect and I'd like to ask you some questions about Jack Doyle's whereabouts at the time of the murder. We can either do it here or down at the station. Your choice."

I reluctantly agreed to come to the police station on Monday. I wanted the weekend to talk to Jack. The thought of an interrogation by Gleason about Marie's murder without knowing exactly what Jack was hiding terrified me. And he *was* hiding something. What worried me was that whatever it was would prove beneficial to Gleason's case against him.

CHAPTER TEN

JACK

I found the Delta Chi frat house on the corner of NE 47th and 20th Avenue NE. It was a stately two-story brick building with white Doric columns in the front that shouted privilege. The house made the places where I lived while attending community college look like homeless squats. The difference rankled me. I've always had to scrabble damn hard for what I wanted while others seem to take their advantages in life for granted. Kate says I have a chip on my shoulder, but I have no problem with being wealthy. I would gladly join the ranks of the one percenters in this country if I could. No, it's the sense of entitlement that characterizes so many of the upper-class elites that gets to me. I have no idea how Kate can deal with the rich and powerful on a regular basis.

Except for an occasional car that passed by, the activity level in the neighborhood was almost non-existent. No dogs barking, no sprinklers swishing, no students with backpacks milling about, no one tossing a frisbee, no loud music or wild parties blaring from inside the houses—just an unnatural stillness. It suddenly occurred to me that the fraternity and sorority houses might not be open during summer term. That would account for the deserted feel to the street. With nothing to lose, I walked up to the front door and knocked. Getting no response, I rapped the brass door knocker more forcefully. I spotted a doorbell to the left of the door and pushed it repeatedly. I was about to give up when a male voice yelled, "Would someone get the damn door!"

Moments later, a petite coed with a mass of curly blonde hair, blue eyes and an angelic face opened the door. I paused a beat to register her unexpected presence. "I thought this was a frat house," I blurted finally.

"It is," she said, rolling her eyes.

"But what—"

"Am I doing here?" she asked, finishing my question.

"Uh, right."

She tossed her shoulder-length hair away from her face, but the curls bounced right back. Frowning, she pulled a colorful scrunchy band from a pocket in her form fitting shorts and, in a matter of seconds, had tied the curls into a ponytail. Noting that I was still waiting for an explanation, she sighed deeply as if it was the millionth time she'd been asked the question. "Some of the houses rent their rooms out in the summer to female students," she said in a weary voice.

"So, the female students get door duty?"

"And any other chores that the guys think are beneath them."

"Sounds like a sexist arrangement, but a nice one for the men in the house."

The blonde flashed a coy smile. "I didn't say the women actually *do* the chores."

"Right. But you *did* open the door, so maybe you can help me."

"Maybe," she shrugged. "What do you want?"

"I'm looking for a student named Rod Dutton. I was told he was a member of the Delta Chi fraternity."

"Never heard of him," she said, tucking a stray curl behind her ear.

"Well, could you ask some of the men in the fraternity if they know him?"

She heaved another deep sigh. "I suppose."

"Thank you," I said. "May I wait inside?" It had begun to rain, and, despite the covered porch, I was still getting wet from an occasional wind gust.

"No can do. I have no idea who you are, and all guests have to be registered ahead of time in the Guest Log."

I'd grown tired of our going nowhere conversation and snapped, "Fine, I'll just wait on the porch while you go find someone who can help me."

She slammed the door shut, clearly indicating her distaste for the task I'd given her. Or maybe it was just me. My usually reliable charms seem to be wasted on the college-age females I'd encountered recently. I waited a few minutes to see if I'd misjudged her. Meanwhile the rain turned into a full-blown storm.

Just when I thought my only good suit would be ruined if I stayed outside any longer, the front door opened. A tall, blond male with a bad case of bed hair stood in front of me with one hand on the door frame for support. I knew a fellow hangover sufferer when I saw him, but it was the stale whiskey stink that left no doubt as to his condition. He wore jeans but no shoes or shirt. "You lookin' for Rod?" he mumbled.

I was momentarily distracted by six-pack abs on full display. Not even when I was young and fit did I ever look that good shirtless. "Yes," I said, quickly refocusing on why I'd come. "Do you know him? I was told he's a Delta Chi man."

"That's right, but he isn't here right now."

"Do you know where he is?

The student yawned and stretched his muscular bare arms above his head. "What day is this?" he asked.

"Friday," I said. "Why?"

"Because Rod volunteers at a food bank on Fridays."

"Do you know the name of the food bank?"

"Uh, give me a minute. I just got up and my brain's a little fuzzy." He flashed me a sheepish grin. "Wicked party last night. I guess I'm still wasted."

I nodded sympathetically but wanted to shake him. There were several food banks in the city, and I didn't want to search all of them. Not in this downpour.

"I got it!" he said, proudly.

"Care to share it with me.? I was relieved that his brain cells still functioned—more or less.

"Sorry, man. The food bank is at that church he goes to . . .what's it called?" He scratched his head, which apparently helped jog his memory. "Oh, yeah. St. Charles on 50th street."

I knew the St. Charles Catholic Church. Kate and I had been members there when we were students. We met at a dance in the church basement. The night was a bust by the time I got there. The guys outnumbered the girls who'd shown up at the dance and there's nothing worse than going to a dance and not getting to dance. I tried cutting in a time or two but once a guy had a partner, he refused to let her go. My buddies had given up and had already split. Drinking beer at our favorite bar seemed a much better option than sipping weak punch and standing around like a wallflower. So, I headed for the door shortly after my arrival.

I like to think that what happened next was fate. Kate calls it a fluke. I'd just opened the door to leave when I collided with a girl on her way inside. She tumbled to the floor and landed flat on her rear end. I rushed to help her, but she waved off my assistance. "I'm all right," she insisted, clearly embarrassed. A rosy glow spread across her perfect face as she gracefully pulled herself upright. Then she smiled at me and I was a goner. "Sorry about that," she said. It wasn't the entrance I'd hoped to make!"

I wasn't usually at a loss for words, but I was so stunned by her beauty that I was practically mute. So many questions raced through my mind: who was she, why had I never seen her before, did she attend St. Charles, and most importantly, did she have a boyfriend? I decided then and there that I would marry her. But it took many weeks and all my considerable charms to convince Kate to even date me, let alone marry me. The biggest mistake of my life was losing the only woman I've ever loved.

St. Charles hadn't changed much over the years. The food bank hadn't been in operation when we took our marriage vows there. The basement where our dances were held had been converted to a large pantry. The brief summer storm had blown over by then, so I waited outside until the last of the people in line had left with their food supplies. Once inside, I spotted Rod Dutton right away. He was the youngest volunteer and the only male present. He had just taken a partially empty box of canned goods off a folding table when I approached. "Excuse me," I said.

He stacked the box on a nearby shelf and greeted me with a smile. "I'm sorry, but the food bank is closed now."

"I'm not here for food," I said, extending my hand. I'm Jack Doyle. May I talk to you for a moment?"

Dutton shook my hand and told me his name. I was encouraged by his friendly and open demeanor. His reddish-brown hair was neatly trimmed and went well with his conservative attire—pressed brown slacks and starched white shirt with the sleeves rolled up to his elbows. He'd loosened a brown tie that had seen better days. He was taller than my six-foot frame but had a much leaner build. "Talk about what?" he asked with a puzzled frown.

I took out my wallet and showed him my P.I. identification. "I'm investigating the murder of Marie Talbot."

Dutton's demeanor instantly changed from friendly to wary. "I don't know anything about that," he said.

"But you were her boyfriend, weren't you?"

"For a while."

"A *while*?" I said with eyebrows raised. "Didn't you date Marie all through high school and your entire freshman year in college as well?"

"How do you know that?" he asked.

"I told you that I'm a private investigator."

Dutton stared at me for an uncomfortable moment, as if debating whether to refute what I'd said. His reluctance to admit to the length of his relationship with Marie struck me as odd. What did he have to gain?

"Okay, you're right," he finally admitted. "Marie and I had been together for a long time."

"Her death must have hit you hard."

"What do you think?" he shot back. Gone was the friendly guy I'd met earlier. But Dutton's anger quickly turned to sorrow. He made the sign of the cross, bowed his head, and began to pray softly. I only caught snatches of his words: *Hail, Mary, full of grace . . .The Lord is with thee . . .Holy Mary, Mother of God, pray for us sinners now and at the hour of our death*. When he ended the prayer, he wiped tears that streamed down his pale face with the back of his hand. "I loved her," he murmured.

Maybe he did love her, but his reaction struck me as way over the top. "All the more reason to talk to me. Marie hired me, and her death has hit me hard too. I'm determined to find her killer. You'd like that, wouldn't you?"

"But the police--"

I cut him off quickly. "I used to be a homicide detective for many years. I know how they work. There are rules and procedures that they have to follow which often just get in the way of solving a case fast. As a P.I., I must follow the law, but I don't have any bureaucrats breathing down my neck to tell me how to do my job." I looked him straight in the eyes. "Marie deserves justice," I said solemnly. "You'd like that, wouldn't you?"

He nodded.

"Then talk to me. The more I know about Marie, the more I'll understand what happened to her and why."

"Okay," Dutton said. "But can we talk while I unload the tables and stack the boxes?" He looked at the two gray-haired women busily counting the items still on the pantry shelves. "The ladies depend on me for the heavy stuff."

"Not a problem," I said, grabbing a box. "I'm good with the heavy stuff, too." As I helped him take down the folding tables I explained why Marie had hired me.

"She said someone was stalking her."

"Stalking Marie?" His surprised reaction suggested he thought the notion highly unlikely.

"That's what she claimed, but the curious part is that she'd already hired another P.I before talking to me."

"Maybe he wasn't making any headway or concluded that there was no stalker. I take it that you believed her, though. Do you think the stalker killed her?"

We carried all the folding tables to the holding rack in a storage closet. "Could be the killer or someone else entirely," I said.

"But I can't imagine why anyone would want to kill Marie. Everyone liked her."

"That's what I've been told." I stopped to wipe sweat from my forehead. The basement was uncomfortably hot and stuffy. "Tell me this, Rod, why did you and Marie break up?"

CONCIERGE AFFAIRS

He shrugged but said nothing.

"I've heard that she was popular with the guys and dumped you to date others. Did that make you jealous?"

"That's a lie! It wasn't like that at all," he insisted. "Marie and I had already begun to drift apart when she started dating others."

"What do you mean by drift apart?"

"You know, like we didn't have the same interests or values anymore.

I'm a sociology major and she was studying engineering. We're both Catholics, but she left the church at the beginning of this year. Both of us used to volunteer at the food bank, but she quit midway through our sophomore year."

"Did she say why?"

"Not really. She just started attending one of those mega churches in Redmond. I think she got wrapped up in some of their programs."

The only Redmond mega church I'd heard about was the Holy Fellowship and that was because there'd been some controversy associated with it. Something to do with parking and traffic issues in the neighborhood. "Are you talking about the church called the Holy Fellowship?" I asked.

Dutton grimaced. "Yeah, that's the one," he said, sullenly.

After we'd finished storing the tables, one of the lady volunteers handed us both a glass of lemonade. "You look like you could use a cold drink," she said. Turning to me she added," Bless you for helping out today."

"My pleasure, ma'am," I said.

"We'll have to lock up as soon as you're finished with your drinks," she added firmly.

"No worries," Dutton assured her.

"I have one last question, Rod. I understand Marie was well-liked, but do you know of anyone who didn't get along with her or argued with her lately? Or maybe there was some guy who wanted to date her and got rejected?"

"I don't know about any dating issues, but she and her brother didn't get along at all."

"Her brother?" Marie had never mentioned a brother.

"Dirk Trstenjak. Half-brother, actually. He's a senior at U-Dub this year. Marie avoided him whenever possible. I think she was afraid of him."

At that point the volunteer lady collected our now empty glasses, thanked us again, and politely shooed us out the door.

I checked my cell phone as soon as I left the church, but the rain had kicked in again and I had to dash to my car. Welcome to summer in Seattle. One of these days I'm going to get smart and buy an umbrella. I'd missed a call from Kate while I was at the food bank, but I was too eager to talk to her to waste time listening to her message. When she didn't answer I left her a message to call me back straightaway. Phone tag was not a game I liked, especially since my cell desperately needed a charge and I didn't have a charger handy. The rain had turned into a harsh downpour by this point, so I decided to just sit in the car until Kate called or the rain tapered off—or my cell died, whichever came first.

I wanted to get Kate's take on my conversation with Rod Dutton—the ex-boyfriend, sociology major, and charity volunteer. I valued her opinion about whether what I'd learned raised any red flags for her. Did she think the breakup with Marie was a red flag? Dutton made it sound like the split was no big deal, but I don't buy it. Not given how long they'd been an item. And not given the way he teared up when he confessed that he still loved her. Was he crying over his former lover's brutal murder or feeling guilty about his part in it? Was his seemingly pious prayer a sincere reaction to her death or just an act?

He did come across as a nice, clean-cut, and helpful guy. Those traits, however, were not enough to let him off my suspect list. All too often it's the nice, clean-cut guy who turns out to be a killer. Ted Bundy comes to mind. The troubled relationship between Marie and her half-brother, on the other hand, was a giant red flag I needed to pursue, with or without Kate's input.

CHAPTER ELEVEN

KATE

The first thing I noticed about Marie's and Alicia's apartment was that it wasn't an apartment. Regent Plaza was an upscale, newly constructed condominium in one of Redmond's most highly desirable neighborhoods. There had been a surge of apartment complexes like theirs built in Redmond over the last few years which catered to young, highly compensated professionals employed by Microsoft and other technology companies. This was no neighborhood for university students on a limited budget. Unless Alicia Gonzales had access to more funds than Marie supposedly had, there was just no way I could envision them living in Regent Plaza.

The ten-story building had an industrial style exterior. The look didn't appeal to me, but it seemed to be the preferred design in new construction these days. A walkway lined with solar light fixtures led to the entrance. Some colorful flowers or greenery would have helped to negate the cold, impersonal feel of the structure. There were two security cameras strategically placed to avoid blind spots for recording any activity near the glass-paneled front door. A doorbell panel listed the names of the condo's occupants. I wasn't entirely sure that I'd come to the right place, so I scanned the panel for Alicia's or Marie's name. Sure enough, there was a listing for M. Talbot and A. Gonzales at Unit 801. I rang the bell and waited. I still didn't know what I'd say if Alicia answered the bell. Jack was ridiculously optimistic about my abilities. Did he really think I could waltz right in and quickly bond with Alicia over motorcycles? Why would she? I was a total stranger to her. Unless I had a burst of inspiration to convince her otherwise, I doubted she'd even buzz me into the building, let alone into her unit.

I waited a while longer and was about to leave when a well-dressed couple came up the walkway. Their loud angry voices suggested that they were engaged in a heated argument that rivaled any feud between the Hatfields and McCoys. They didn't seem to notice or care that I witnessed their battle. The female I tagged as 'Hatfield' stopped shrieking long enough to slide a magnetic card into a slotted reader. When the door opened, I quickly slipped behind and followed them into the lobby. The couple continued their verbal barrage as they headed for the elevator. From what I knew about multi-story condominiums, the elevator probably required a key card as well. When the vacant elevator arrived, I again followed them. Once inside, the duo finally registered my presence with a perfunctory nod. The male I dubbed 'McCoy' swiped his card and punched a button marked *Six*. Turning to me, he asked, "What floor?"

"Eight," I replied.

He held out his hand for my security card. I was afraid of this exact possibility. Like many of the luxury condos I was familiar with, security was taken seriously. Each floor required a unique card to correspond to the floor on which they resided. Since the couple's card only accessed their sixth floor, I needed my own card to send the elevator to the eighth floor. I suppose it was an effective security measure, but it made visiting friends on any floor besides your own difficult at best. Thinking fast, I rummaged through my handbag. "Oh, no," I cried. "I can't find my card. I think I may have lost it."

Hatfield shot me a disgusted look, but McCoy said, "No problem. There's a little trick I discovered by accident that will work just as well. Do you have a credit card with your name on it?"

I opened my wallet and handed my Visa card to him. He swiped the card and then pushed the button for the eighth floor. The elevator doors promptly closed, and we were on our way. "Thank you so much," I said, sighing in genuine relief. His trick had worked and there weren't any pesky security cameras in the elevator to record the incident.

When he handed my credit card back, Hatfield chided him. "You're going to get into trouble one of these days for doing that."

He shrugged his shoulders and said, "Like you'd care if I did." After that exchange the couple glared at each other without further comment. As soon as they exited the elevator on floor six, they began to rant at each other again.

Now that I had successfully entered the building and had bypassed elevator security to arrive at Alicia's floor, I had one more problem to overcome—what could I possibly say that would convince her to invite me inside her unit? I paused in front of the door to unit 801 and struggled to think of some magic words. It was useless. My mind was a total blank. I should have anticipated the problem before I'd set out on this dubious mission. Forget talking to Alicia about Marie. I'd have to tell Jack that I couldn't even get inside her front door.

"Who are you?" came a voice behind me.

I turned around and there stood Alicia. I assumed it was her since she resembled Jack's description perfectly—tattoos, piercings, purple hair, scowly face and all. She held a grocery bag in one hand and a key chain with several keys attached in the other.

"Oh. Hi, there," I said. "I'm Kate. Are you Alicia?"

She ignored my greeting and focused her piercing dark eyes on the pin I'd fastened to my blouse at the last minute. I hadn't worn the pin in ages, so it had taken me several minutes to find it. It was a simple piece of jewelry—just two letter Bs in fancy script studded with diamond chips. A tiny motorcycle dangled from the two letters on a short silver chain.

Alicia's scowly face had softened a bit as she stared at the pin. After a moment she turned her attention to my face. "Are you one of the Biker Belles?" she asked.

"You've heard of the Belles?"

Alicia rolled her eyes. "Of course! Every female biker has heard of the Belles."

She was probably right. The Belles had gained some notoriety for clever motorcycle stunts and fancy costumes. We performed at all the big biking events. "Yes, I admitted. I was a Belle."

She looked me over carefully as if unconvinced. "You don't look like a biker chick."

I chuckled. "Well, we come in all shapes and sizes. Strange as it may seem, I *was* a Biker Belle—but it was a long time ago. I had a modified Shadow VT700. What do you ride?"

The scowl was back. "I got hit by a fuckin' semi, totaled my Harley and almost lost my leg. I'm just a gimpy bicycle rider now."

"I'm so sorry to hear that. I've had my share of road rash. I went down on a bad patch of black ice and broke just about every bone in my body. I haven't ridden since."

And just like that we were inside her unit drinking beer and bonding over stories about riding the wind. The more we talked, the more she seemed to relax. Her scowly demeanor was long gone. She even cracked a smile a time or two. Despite our apparent differences, a mutual love of riding was a definite ice breaker. I guess Jack was right after all.

Alicia never once asked me why I showed up at her door until I finally steered the conversation around to what I'd really come to talk about: Marie Talbot. "This is a really nice condo you have, Alicia." It had a spacious and open floor plan that allowed an unobstructed view of the kitchen with top-of-the-line stainless-steel appliances, marble countertops, and a selection of fancy electronic gadgets I couldn't begin to identify. The separate dining and living rooms were like a model home display of high-end Danish design furnishings. Not an IKEA table, beanbag chair, or cinder block bookcase in sight. "Do you live here by yourself?" I asked.

Alicia frowned and popped the cap on her third bottle of beer. She offered me another round, but I'd already reached my limit and declined. I munched on the chips and dip she'd put out on the coffee table earlier and waited for her to answer. It's always tempting to fill in the silence with another question or comment when someone doesn't respond right away. But I've found that it's always better to just keep quiet. It doesn't usually take long for the other person to break the uncomfortable silence.

"Yeah," she said. "I used to have a roommate, but she was killed recently."

"Oh, no," I said. "That's horrible! What happened?" I felt a little awkward not letting on that I knew all about Marie's death.

"She was murdered. Pushed off the roof of a high-rise, actually."

"That must have been a terrible shock for you."

Alicia took a big gulp of beer and then belched. "I didn't believe it at first," she said. "Not until the police came knocking on our door."

"I can understand that," I said. "A good friend of mine just lost her niece in the same way and . . . wait a minute. Are we talking about Marie Talbot?"

"I guess so, if that was the name of your friend's niece. She was the perfect roommate and friend." Alicia glanced toward the front door. "I keep expecting her to come bouncing in at any moment."

"Tell me about her," I said. From what my friend said, Marie was well liked by everyone."

"That's why I can't figure out who'd want to kill her. We went to high school together and she was always doing something good for others. I used to get bullied a lot because of my limp and Marie always stood up for me. She's the reason I'm even in college."

"What do you mean?"

"I was in a bad place after the accident. Like suicidal. When the settlement check for the accident finally came in, I went out every night and got wasted. I had the money to buy the best Harley on the market, but I was too messed up to care." I was in a downward spiral to oblivion until Marie stepped in. She convinced me that the accident was a blessing in disguise." Alicia fingered one of her pierced ears. "Not many of the gang I rode with knew that I was a top student. I mean, look at me. Who would think I was college material?"

"I bet Marie did," I said.

"You got it. She encouraged me to use the settlement to pay for college instead of throwing it away on booze and drugs. Marie turned my life around."

I smiled and said, "She was a very good friend."

"Yeah, she was," Alicia said, eyes downcast.

"But there's something I don't understand. I know Marie attended U-Dub on a scholarship and you said the settlement is paying your college expenses."

"So?"

I waved a hand at the apartment's furnishings. Most college students can't afford a condo like this, particularly in one of Redmond's most expensive neighborhoods."

Alicia laughed. "Yeah, it's a trip, isn't it? Two poor girls from Yakima go to college in style."

"How is that possible?"

"That's the thing. I don't know for sure. This condo was Marie's doing. Now that she's gone, I'll have to move out. My settlement was substantial but not enough to live like this."

"How did Marie pay for the condo?"

"She never said. Just told me everything was covered and not to worry about it and I didn't. I trusted her."

"Hmm. Did she have a rich relative helping her out?"

"Not that I know of." Alicia flashed a cheeky grin. "I always suspected Marie had a sugar daddy."

"Who do you think he was?"

Alicia's scowl was back. "What's with all the questions about Marie?" Before I could answer, she stood upright but seemed a little off balance, either from the beer or her leg. She leaned on the back of her chair for support and snarled, "You already knew Marie was my roommate. "Are you a cop?"

I'd overplayed my hand. "No, absolutely not," I assured her.

"Don't tell me you're a private investigator. I've already been down that road and it wasn't pretty."

"No, not a P.I."

"A reporter?"

"No."

"Then just exactly why *are* you here?"

Her glare was unnerving, but I came up with an excuse that seemed reasonable—at least to me. "You're right," I said. I did know that you and Marie were roommates. I also know that when someone close to you is killed, it often helps to talk about them with a caring individual. Marie's aunt was eager to talk about her niece and thanked me for listening. I thought you might appreciate a sympathetic listener, too."

Alicia reacted to my little speech as if I'd told her to eat all her spinach because it was good for her. "That's a load of crap! I don't know what you're trying to sell here, lady, but I'm not interested. Go knock on someone else's door. There's a poor geezer down the hall whose wife just kicked the bucket. Didn't you know about that?" She looked at me as if seeing me for the first time. "Come to think of it, I've never seen you around here before. Do you live on this floor?"

I may shade the truth from time to time, but I refuse to outright lie. I shook my head, knowing what was surely coming next. And Alicia delivered.

"Do you even *live* in the building?"

Again, I shook my head.

"How did you know I was Marie's roommate or where we lived?"

"Look, Alicia, I've obviously upset you and that certainly wasn't my intention."

"Get out!" she demanded, pointing to the door. Her face had flushed a mottled red and her body trembled. "You're nothing but a ghoulish bitch," she yelled. "A bitch who gets off on other people's grief!"

I stood and apologized, but she was too enraged to listen.

"OUT NOW!!"

The situation was beyond salvaging, so I had no choice but to leave. Staying any longer would've been unwise and possibly dangerous. Injured leg or not, Alicia looked perfectly capable of committing great bodily harm. *Thanks for the heads up, Jack.*

As I walked out the door, she taunted, "I bet you've never been on a bike in your life!"

CHAPTER TWELVE

JACK

When Kate and I finally connected by phone and she told me that Kevin Gleason had shown up on her doorstep, my blood pressure went through the roof. I spewed a few choice expletives, which felt good but did nothing to ease my frustration. "What did the conniving a-hole want?" I asked, between curses.

"Calm down, Jack," Kate said. "Knock off the outrage and I'll tell you."

"Okay, okay." Kate had little tolerance for profanity. "I apologize for the foul language." I paused, took a deep breath, and mustered the nicest tone that I could without gagging. "What did Detective Kevin Gleason want?"

"Thank you," she said. "He wanted to come inside my apartment and ask me some questions."

"Tell me you didn't let him inside!"

"Of course not. But then he asked me to come down to the station for an interview."

"He wasn't interested in talking to you before. What's changed?"

"He didn't say."

"Probably just a fishing expedition. If he asks again, tell him no. You have that right."

"He said I'd have to cooperate, or he'd serve me with a material witness warrant."

"Empty threat."

"Maybe, but I agreed to an interview at the station on Monday."

"Kate, why on God's green earth would you do that?"

"I really didn't have a choice. You know the man. He's like a dog after a bone; he'll pester me until he gets what he wants."

Dejected, I sighed and said, "I know. Just be careful, Kate. I can guarantee that Gleason will try to manipulate you. He's skilled at tricking adversaries into saying something that will come back to bite them—in this case, me and possibly you."

"That's why I think we should get together and talk first. I have some questions of my own I'd like you to answer before I meet with him."

Since summer was summer again, we decided to take advantage of the sunny day before the rains came back. We agreed to meet at Bellevue City Park later in the afternoon. Kate had a training session scheduled with a new hire and would be tied up until after lunch. That gave me enough time to see a dog about a bone.

****

Although I've never ventured inside Seattle Police Headquarters, I've spent plenty of time outside the building since becoming a P.I. I'm always on the lookout for new clients, and police personnel can be good referral sources. I do the same thing at the Columbia Center, where a ton of lawyers have their offices. I've handed out a lot of business cards with *nada* results so far. I don't know whether it's personal or if it's because private investigators don't generally have a good reputation. I'm guilty of dissing P.I.s when I was a cop. To me, they were all cheating-husband-chasers who thought they were real detectives. The worst were those who butted into official police investigations. Obviously, I've reassessed the P.I. role.

Once I cleared the metal detector, I consulted a wall directory to find the floor for the homicide unit. The city is divided geographically into several precincts, but all the homicide detectives work out of the headquarters facility as do detectives assigned to various other units such as robbery, missing persons, and emergency response. Although it was Saturday, I figured Gleason would be on duty. Marie's case had attracted a lot of media attention and there was public pressure to quickly solve her murder. I stopped at the duty desk and told the officer I'd come to see Detective Gleason.

"What is this regarding, sir?" he asked. The silver-haired officer was in his sixties and spoke with a posh English accent.

"Just let him know that Jack Doyle is here."

As I expected, it didn't take but a New York minute for Gleason to barrel through an unmarked door. "Doyle," he smirked, "it's so nice of you to visit us at last."

"You knew I'd come in if you harassed Kate."

"I'd hardly call it harassment. I was just doing my job. Detectives ask questions, don't you remember? And Kate was a witness to Marie Talbot's death. I have relevant questions to ask her."

"Leave Kate out of this, Gleason. She doesn't know anything about what happened to Marie."

He smiled without a trace of mirth. "But she knows you, Doyle." He opened the unmarked door and said, "Follow me." We walked down a long hallway and passed by a room with a series of partitions that functioned as privacy screens between detectives' desks. I had the same office setup in the BPD. Gleason dumped me in an interview room and left to gather the case file before starting the interview. I decided there were three ways I could play our so-called interview today—angrily, civilly or treat it like the joke it was. I chose the third way. "I could use some coffee," I said. "Bring me back a cup, will ya?" The look Gleason gave me was blistering. "Be sure you add sugar and cream," I added with a dimpled grin.

The interview room was like all the others I'd been in over the years—cramped and smelled of B.O. and fear. The scuffed white walls could have used some fresh paint and the two-way mirror needed a small crack repaired. The only furniture was a wooden table and metal chairs. One side of the table had a single chair for the interviewee while the other side had two chairs in case two detectives conducted the interview. I sat on the detectives' side.

Half an hour later, Gleason returned with a woman whom he introduced as his partner, Detective Lucy Miller. She was younger, taller and definitely more good-looking than Gleason. She wore her short brown hair in a saucy bob and had a model's slim figure. Her cornflower blue eyes looked me over carefully as she handed me the cup of coffee I'd requested. I thanked her with a grateful smile and then asked, "Did Detective Gleason have you brew the coffee as well as serve it? A red flush spread across Gleason's face, which I took as a yes. He slapped the case folder on the table and barked, "Get your butt to the other side of the table."

"Sorry," I said, grinning. "Force of habit."

After the detectives settled themselves on their side of the table, Gleason began the interview by turning on a recorder with a remote control. He then stated who was present, the date, time, and a couple of other standard phrases for the record. "Now," he said, "let's discuss your movements on the day of the murder."

"That's kind of personal, but okay . . . I usually have a movement right after I get out of bed in the morning. I'm very regular."

I caught a slight upturn of Miller's lips, but Gleason didn't appreciate my humor. "Can the funny business, Doyle," he snapped. "This is a serious interview."

"Right," I agreed. "And for the record, I am here voluntarily."

Gleason cleared his throat. "We have a witness who saw Marie Talbot enter your apartment building on June 24 at 9:00 a.m. Approximately ten minutes later she fell to her death. Minutes after her fall you sprinted full speed out of your building. Why were you in such a hurry?"

"I was late for an appointment."

"An appointment with Marie Talbot at Java Joe's?"

"That's correct."

"If you were going to meet at Java Joe's, why did she tell the security guard on duty that she was headed to a meeting with you at your apartment?"

"I have no idea."

"Did she come to your apartment?"

"No."

"Did you see her in the building?"

"No."

"Why were you late to your appointment with her at Java Joe's?"

"I got held up by a phone call."

"A phone call? From whom?"

"The identity of the person is irrelevant to your case."

"You know that we can check your phone records."

"Go for it. The records will verify that I was still on the phone when Marie fell off the roof."

Miller spoke for the first time. "What was your relationship with Miss Talbot?"

"She was a potential client."

Miller flipped through the case folder until she found the paper she needed. "According to our file, Miss Talbot had already signed an agreement with Arnold DuPont. Why would she need to hire you?"

I shrugged and sipped my lukewarm coffee. "Any number of reasons, I suppose."

"What sort of reasons?"

"Maybe DuPont wasn't making enough progress, or she couldn't afford his outrageous fees, I don't know. What I do know is that she told a trusted friend that she needed someone to find out who was stalking her. The friend referred her to me."

"The trusted friend being Tom Lamont, your building's security guard."

"Correct."

"But she hadn't hired you yet."

I nodded. "Correct again."

"Is it also correct that you had a romantic relationship with Miss Talbot."

I spit out a mouthful of coffee. "What?"

Gleason had a snarky, "gotcha" look plastered on his face.

"Answer the question, Mr. Doyle," Miller said. "Were you and Miss Talbot romantically involved?"

Her line of questioning was absurd, but she had succeeded in rattling me. I dabbed at the spilled coffee with my handkerchief. Miller accused me of stalling and told me again to answer the question. "No! Of course not!" I said.

"Hmm," she said, removing a photograph from the folder. "Do you know what this is?" she asked, sliding the photograph across the desk.

"It appears to be an ultrasound scan."

"An ultrasound scan of a baby. The scan has been identified by Miss Talbot's physician as belonging to her."

"Marie was pregnant?" *I had a sinking feeling that I knew where this interview was headed.*

"The medical examiner has confirmed she was eleven weeks along."

"That's news to me."

"Come on, Doyle," Gleason said. "You knew perfectly well she was pregnant. She never wanted to hire you for some bullshit stalking case. Marie Talbot was your lover and was going to have your baby. A baby you didn't want."

I scooted the chair back and stood up. "I'm done here."

"Not so fast, Doyle. We need you to submit to a DNA test."

"I'm not submitting to anything without consulting my lawyer first." *A lawyer I don't have and can't afford.*

Gleason sneered triumphantly. "Of course. That's your right."

CHAPTER THIRTEEN

KATE

Jack was already at the park when I arrived. He sat on a bench near the soccer field eating a hot dog stuffed with mustard, onions, and sauerkraut. "I would've bought you one," he said, "but I didn't think you would eat it."

"Not in a million years!" I said, laughing. I took a Tupperware container, fork and water bottle out of my handbag. "Fortunately, I have an arugula salad with salmon."

Jack feigned disgust with a gagging gesture. "There's just no accounting for taste," he said, shaking his head.

Jack had dressed casually today in khaki cargo shorts, polo shirt, and sport shoes. The look was more his style than the spiffy suit he'd been wearing since becoming a P.I. I liked the change in attire, despite the glob of mustard that stained his shirt. Aside from his eating and drinking habits, I couldn't deny that Jack still appealed to me. I tried mightily to ignore these fleeting instances of insanity whenever they unexpectedly popped up. There was just something endearing about the man today, mustard stain and all, that pierced my resolve. Again.

He eyed my water bottle. "You have another one of those?" he asked. "I'd have brought some beer for us, but the park doesn't allow alcohol."

What a pity. I handed him my spare water bottle and watched as he chugged half of it down in one big thirsty gulp. "Ah," he sighed. "That tasted almost as good as a pint of Guinness." Alcohol and Jack have a love affair that is still going strong after many attempted breakups. If we didn't solve Marie's murder before Gleason found a trumped-up reason to arrest Jack, I was afraid the romance would be permanent.

Jack finished his hotdog in a couple of quick bites and didn't say anything while I ate my salad. The silence was deafening. Jack was a talker. I've seen him initiate a conversation in a crowded elevator, in line at the grocery store, in a doctor's waiting room—basically, anywhere he could make a connection with people. I think he saw it as a challenge, especially if he came across a bleary-eyed, coffee-deprived office worker or someone whose demeanor was unfriendly or standoffish. Then Jack would pull out all the stops. He'd flash his dimpled grin and draw upon his repertoire of Irish blarney until he got them to interact with him—happily or not.

Jack's silence was disturbing. His eyes had lost their usual sparkle and reflected the sullen mood he now projected. Granted, he had a lot on his mind, but Jack was generally an upbeat kind of guy. Until he hit a roadblock. And Jack had hit a double whammy—a P.I. career that was going nowhere and Gleason's single-minded effort to pin Marie Talbot's murder on him. We both knew where those setbacks could lead.

He focused intently on the park and its environs as if he were on a stakeout. "Are you expecting someone to join us?" I asked.

"No," he said after a long pause. "Just people-watching."

The sunny day after the recent rainstorm was a welcome respite that had enticed a lot of visitors to the park. The bench where we sat was a perfect spot for people-watching; there were picnickers, mothers with baby strollers, Tai Chi exercisers, joggers and walkers, and a soccer game in progress. Excited children jumped, ran, and swung on playground equipment. No homeless persons or drug dealers in sight. In short, it was a typical downtown park in white bread Bellevue.

I finished my lunch and watched Jack for a few minutes. I had a feeling that his people-watching was just an excuse to avoid talking about what was on his mind. Something had happened that bothered him, and I refused to let him stall any longer.

I waved my hand to get his attention. "Hello, there. We need to talk."

He shrugged.

"What's wrong, Jack? You seem like you're troubled."

"Nope," he said, "not at all."

Liar, I thought but didn't say. Jack tossed his lunch wrappers into a trash can and swigged more water. He uncrossed his long legs and re-tied a loose shoestring. Then he sat upright, straightened his shoulders and took a deep breath. It seemed like an attempt to shake off whatever he'd been quietly thinking. "How'd you get on with Alicia Gonzales?" he asked at last.

"You were right about the motorcycle connection. It got me into her condo and kick started our conversation."

He smiled for the first time today. "See, I knew you'd bond with her. Learn anything?"

"I know all about her bike, the accident and how much she admired Marie . . ."

"I hear a *but* coming."

"But I asked one too many questions about Marie and she suddenly grew suspicious of my motives. You told me she could be intimidating, but not what to expect if she got riled up."

"Yeah, I should've warned you that might happen. I didn't talk to her very long, but long enough to conclude that Alicia Gonzales is tightly wired and easily riled." He offered me a wan smile which I took as an apology. "Did you find out anything we can use?"

"Maybe. They live in an upscale neighborhood in Redmond and their condo looks like a showroom, very modern with expensive furnishings."

"How do they afford it?"

"Alicia had a settlement for her accident that pays her college expenses, but the condo and its furnishings came courtesy of Marie."

"What do you make of that?"

"Alicia said she suspected Marie had a sugar daddy who foot the bills."

"Hmm," he said. "That would certainly explain their living conditions. I don't suppose she told you who he was."

"No, and when I asked, she threw me out."

"Do you think Alicia knows his identity?"

"No, but I can't be sure."

A soccer ball escaped from the players nearby and landed in front of our bench. Jack picked up the ball and tossed it to the teen who'd chased after it. "Here ya go, Beckham Junior." When Jack sat down, he asked, "You're around rich folk all the time in your concierge business. Know any likely candidates?"

I laughed. "Sorry, no one comes to mind."

"The only rich dude I know who's connected to the case is Arnold DuPont," Jack said. He rubbed his face and added, "Maybe Marie came to him for help and a relationship developed."

"Possible, I suppose."

"He could even be the father of Marie's—"

"What?"

"Nothing."

"Jack, what were you going to say?"

"Marie was pregnant."

"Pregnant! How do you know that?"

Kevin Gleason and his sidekick told me; even showed me her ultrasound photo they found hidden in her bedroom."

"And you're just now telling me? When did you see Gleason?"

"Yesterday."

"Why, Jack? Why did you change your mind about talking to him? You knew I agreed to go to the station on Monday. Were you afraid I might say something I shouldn't?"

A commotion erupted from the playground that caught our attention. Two little tykes at the monkey bars were in a fight—mostly a noisy shoving and pushing match. Jack raised his voice a couple of notches and said, "No, Kate, I wasn't afraid of what you might say. I wanted to tell Gleason to leave you alone. That you didn't know anything about Marie's murder."

"Do you? I mean, do you know something about the murder? Something that you're not telling me?"

Jack threw his hands in the air. "Jesus, Mary, and Joseph! No!"

"Fine. But you never said why you weren't at Java Joe's for our meeting. You hadn't even left your apartment building until *after* she'd fallen."

"I didn't think it was important, but if you must know, I was late because of a phone call."

"A phone call from whom?"

"Aw, Kate, you're as bad as Gleason. It was just a crank call."

"A crank call made you late. Really? Why didn't you just hang up?"

"Okay, okay. I didn't hang up because the person who called said they had a message for me about Marie. I stayed on the line to listen to the message."

"Was the caller male or female?"

"It was hard to tell. They sounded like they had a cold or stuffed nose. It could've been a heavy smoker's raspy voice."

"What was the message?"

"They went on and on about how Marie wasn't the Goody-Two-Shoes that everyone believed. They called her a slut who slept with rich married men. I hung up at that point."

"Interesting," I said. "This is the first time that we've heard anything negative about Marie."

"*If* it's even true. I don't put much stock in anonymous phone calls."

"How did this person even know your phone number?"

"I've been handing out business cards to anyone and everyone. My number is out there."

"Did you tell Gleason about the call?"

"No, and I don't want you to say anything, either."

"Why not? It might be very relevant, especially given that a sugar daddy might be in the mix."

"Gleason's sidekick, Detective Lucy Miller, accused me of being the father of Marie's baby. Said I killed her because I didn't want a baby."

"Oh, my God! That's ridiculous."

"Exactly. They want me to take a DNA test."

"That's good!" I exclaimed. "It will prove that you're not the father."

"I put them off. Said I had to consult with my lawyer first."

"Why? I would think you'd jump at the chance to prove them wrong ... unless they're not."

"For God's sake, Kate. You know me. I would never stoop that low. Marie was just a kid!" His sky-blue eyes were wet when they found mine. He took my hands in his and said, "You *have* to believe me, Katie. Marie was just a potential client, that's all.

I wanted to believe him. I truly did.

CHAPTER FOURTEEN

JACK

I blew it. Twice. I should've taken the damn test yesterday. Because I stalled, Kate is questioning my relationship with Marie Talbot. She already believes I've held things back or shaded the truth, which, is sort of true. I can't do it again or, knowing Kate, she will bail on me altogether. Her insights and abilities are better than most experienced cops--including me. Especially since I'm barely keeping it together these days. If I were at the top of my game, I wouldn't be so desperate for her help. But I need Kate on my team if I'm going to have any chance of solving this case. I also thought that by working the case together we might rekindle the love we once shared. At this point that idea is just a fantasy.

I blew it again in the interview with Gleason and Miller. I didn't take the meeting as seriously as I should have. Gleason and his cohort were able to land a couple of punches which was exactly what I'd warned Kate to guard against. His new partner Lucy Miller proved to be just as devious as Gleason. I was so angry at the way she'd questioned me that I lost it. At that point there was no way I'd agree to anything she wanted me to do.

I'm not worried about the DNA results; I know that I'm not the father of Marie's baby and the test will prove it. They may be onto something about the baby's father, though. A romantic relationship between Marie and DuPont is more believable than an affair with me. I'm flat broke and struggling. DuPont is successful and rich. If Marie did have a sugar daddy, DuPont is a prime candidate. It would certainly explain Marie's luxurious lifestyle. The more I think about it, the more it makes sense. What if the reason Marie came to me for help was because DuPont was her stalker? The scenario could've played out like this: Marie gets pregnant with DuPont's baby. DuPont is afraid that his affair with a client would be revealed publicly. His marriage, career, and reputation are on the line. His solution is to kill Marie at my apartment building to throw suspicion my way. This version of events makes sense. The problem is proving it.

Water is a poor substitute for booze. I needed a *real* drink. Since Murphy's Bar in Seattle was my pub of choice, I bypassed the trendy drinking spots in Bellevue and took the floating bridge over Lake Washington to Seattle.

Although Murphy's isn't technically a sports bar, it did have a big plasma TV mounted on the wall to cater to the Husky and Seahawk fans during football season. It's the Mariners that bring in the summertime crowds. Basketball lost some of its appeal when the Super Sonics went to Oklahoma and became the Oklahoma City Thunder. Golf doesn't have the same draw with Murphy's clientele. That's why I was confused when the big screen had a station tuned to some golf tournament. That no one seemed to care wasn't surprising. The scofflaws who spent the most time at Murphy's were dedicated drinkers and bullshitters. Any sport on TV would do.

I sat down on a stool and ordered my usual pick-me-up. A skinny Black guy in his twenties was behind the counter. His name tag said Buster, but he'd crossed it out and scribbled Jamal in its place. He had no idea what "my usual" was. A regular at the bar who everyone called Nick the Mick, spouted loudly, "He's a newbie. Don't know vodka from gin."

"Thass right," someone else slurred, which prompted the rest of the guys at the counter to get their two cents worth of grumbles in.

"Hey, you losers," I blurted. "Give the guy a break. Alcohol is alcohol. Drink up or shut up." That settled, I smiled at Jamal and ordered a beer instead of whiskey. "Where's Murphy?" I asked Jamal.

"He's at home. Sick with the flu," he said. "Buster usually subs for Murphy, but he had to go to traffic court today."

"How'd you get saddled with the job?"

"I live next door to Murphy, and he was desperate. I don't even have a license or certification," he admitted with a worried look.

"No one here will snitch to the authorities," I assured him. "You'll do just fine. These barflies will chug down anything you put in front of them. But you could do one thing for me."

"Sure. What's that?"

I pointed to the TV. "Change the channel to something worth watching."

As Jamal flipped through the channels, an interview with Seahawk quarterback Russell Wilson caught my attention. Marie's ex-boyfriend said that her brother attended U-Dub on a football scholarship. I thought I'd heard the Trstenjak name before. The Huskies went to the Rose Bowl this year and Dirk made the winning touchdown. I still hadn't talked to him. If Marie was afraid of her brother, I wanted to know why. Was he stalking her? Did he have a motive to kill her?

If there's one thing I know, it's the bar scene in Seattle. Mention a group of people and I can tell you what their favorite pub is. I know where the cops, the blue-collar workers, the professionals, the millennials, the ne'er-do-wells, the college crowd, and most important, where the U-Dub jocks prefer to hang out. When I finished my beer, I headed for The Ave and the bar where I hoped to find Dirk.

The End Zone was mostly empty this afternoon. I grabbed a table near the door and ordered a cheeseburger, fries, and a whiskey sour over ice. I nursed my drink and hoped that Dirk would eventually show up. It was a long shot, but I had nothing else to do. I figured that even if he was a no-show, maybe someone would know where I could find him.

I'd never seen a photo of the Rose Bowl star without his uniform and helmet on, so I turned to Facebook. His home page allowed public access, so I scrolled through the photos he'd posted. It was a selfies extravaganza: Dirk and his teammates, Dirk at the Rose Bowl, Dirk at the gym, Dirk at parties (looking plastered), and Dirk with a variety of coeds—all movie star beautiful. It had to be Dirk's fame that attracted the women because it certainly wasn't his looks. As Kate's Texas friend would say, "He looks like the dog's been keepin' him under the porch."

As time passed and more college kids arrived, I felt out of my element. The End Zone was not the place where people as old as their parents go to drink. I got more than a few curious looks and, occasionally, hostile stares. They probably pegged me as a cop, which happens a lot. That's why I was never assigned to undercover work. When four o'clock rolled around, I took advantage of the Happy Hour prices and ordered some nachos with all the trimmings and a pitcher of beer. I'd just finished the last of the nachos when Dirk and his buddies burst into the bar, laughing and jostling each other like unruly teenagers. There weren't any vacant tables or counter stools by that time and when Dirk spotted me sitting all alone at a table for four, I suddenly had company. "Piss off, Gramps," Dirk said, in a take-no-prisoners stance. His size was intimidating but his voice—a hoarse frog croak—ruined the macho effect. "This table is reserved for me and my peeps."

"Well, if it isn't Dirk Trstenjak," I said, "star of the Rose Bowl. I motioned to an empty chair. "Sit your ass down and I'll overlook the Gramps slur."

"Damn. The old guy's got balls," hooted one of his muscular pals. "He's called you out, man." The others laughed as Dirk's face turned an angry red. "Stuff it, Leon," he growled.

"Hey, it's all cool," I said, smiling with both hands raised in surrender. "Grab a couple more chairs and all your 'peeps' can sit down. "What're you drinking? The first round is on me." Dirk hesitated a moment, shrugged and then sat down, too. Making friends with free booze doesn't work every time, but with college jocks it's practically guaranteed. I just hoped that my credit card would cover the tab, or our so-called friendship would turn ugly quick. As we waited for our drink orders to arrive, Dirk turned his attention to me and asked, "Who are you, man, and what're you doing here?"

"Funny you should ask. I'm Jack Doyle and you called me. I'm here to finish our conversation about your sister."

His bushy eyebrows shot up. "*You're* Jack Doyle? You hung up on me!" he complained indignantly.

"True, but you didn't identify yourself. If you had, I would've stayed on the line. Talking in person is much better, don't you think?"

"How'd you know it was me who called?"

"I didn't until you came to my table and spoke. You have the same hoarse voice as my anonymous caller."

"I've got a bad cold," Dirk said. To emphasize the point, he blew his nose on one of the bar napkins and started coughing. "Can't seem to shake it," he admitted. Just then a server approached our table with the beer we'd ordered. As soon as she set the pitchers on the table, Dirk turned to his buddies and said, "Hey guys, some stools at the counter just opened up. Take two of these pitchers and head on over there. I have some business to discuss with Doyle here."

"Why'd you call me?" I asked after the others had left.

"The newspaper said that Mariji was killed at the building where her P.I. lived. They didn't mention your name, but I have some classes with the security guard at your place. Tom gave me one of your cards."

Good old helpful Tom. You don't seem too upset by your sister's murder."

"Half-sister!" No, I'm not, actually." He wiped his runny nose and then filled his beer glass from the pitcher in front of him. The pitcher was almost empty, so I slid a second pitcher across the table. "Mariji didn't fool me," he said after a couple of gulps. "Everyone thought she could walk on water, but I knew the real Mariji."

"What do you mean?"

"Lissen," he slurred, "Karma's a bitch. Mariji deserved what happened."

I sipped my beer and didn't respond.

"She didn't want any part of our family, which was fine by me. She even changed her name. Mariji was nothing but trouble. She was a little brat when her mom married my dad. I got blamed for everything, but Mariji could do no wrong in his eyes. My dad doted on the bitch."

"You sound like you hated her."

"Hate is not a strong enough word."

"Do you have any idea who might have killed her?"

"Besides me, you mean?"

"Did you?"

He snorted. "She knew how I felt and steered clear of me. And I steered clear of her. Mariji wasn't dumb, just clever. She used her beauty to get whatever she wanted."

"What did she want?"

Dirk rubbed his thumb and fingers together. "Money. Mariji was all about the Benjamins. She dated a lot of the fools on campus, but she was always on the lookout for some rich dude who could give her the good life. She even moved to Redmond so she would have better pickings. She must have done all right because from what I've heard Mariji had hooked up with a married man. A rich married man."

"Do you know who he was?"

Dirk shook his head. "No, but I think it had to be someone from that mega-church in Redmond. It's filled with the mega-rich."

CHAPTER FIFTEEN

KATE

"Kate, thank you so much for coming in today. I know how busy you are with your new business." Gleason's effusive welcome was echoed by his partner.

"Yes," she said. "We very much appreciate your cooperation."

"And you are?" I knew she was Gleason's female partner, but Jack hadn't mentioned how attractive she was or how stylishly she dressed for a detective. She had on a navy-blue designer suit, white silk blouse, gold earrings and open-toed Tory Burch high heels. The heels added at least three inches to her already tall frame. The striking difference between Gleason's diminutive stature and her height was distracting. I pictured them as dance partners and tried not to laugh.

"I'm sorry," Gleason said. "I should've introduced you. This is Detective Lucy Miller, my new partner."

Miller and I shook hands.

"Detective Miller will be conducting your interview today," Gleason said. The pompous way he delivered the announcement reminded me of one of Danielle's favorite sayings, "He thinks the sun come up just to hear him crow." He puffed up his slight chest and confirmed the impression by adding, "My expertise is needed on another important case." Miller rolled her eyes as he hurried off. It seemed his not-so-subtle boast disguised as an explanation didn't impress her any more than it did me. Could it be that Gleason and Miller's partnership was already on shaky ground?

"Follow me," she said. "We can talk in my office. Her "office" turned out to be a small cubicle with a desk and two chairs. There were sound-dampening partitions on three sides that separated it from the other cubicles in the room. The partitions did a good job of muting the noise from phones ringing, keyboards clicking, and scattered conversations. "Would you like something to drink?" Miller asked as I sat down in the chair she indicated. "I don't recommend our coffee, but the soda and bottled water are good choices.

I asked for water and she left to fetch it. When she returned a few minutes later she had a bottle for each of us. Once she'd settled herself behind the desk, she said, "I want to thank you again for agreeing to help us with our inquiries."

"You're welcome, but I really don't know how I can be of any help."

"That's a common misconception by witnesses in an investigation. There may be something that you don't think is important but can be quite significant."

I shrugged and uncapped the water bottle. "Okay."

"I'd like to start by getting some background information." She had a calm, reassuring voice. "Tell me about Jack Doyle. I understand that you were married at one time. What is your relationship with him now?"

"I wouldn't call it a relationship exactly, I said after downing a quick drink of water."

"What would you call it?"

"We share a grown daughter and granddaughter together and, for their sake, we try to keep our interactions with each other amicable."

"How often do you have these amicable interactions?"

"Oh, not often. But we are together as a family on most holidays."

"What about non-holiday occasions?"

"I helped him with a police investigation once. I was concierge at the condominium where a murder took place that he was investigating."

"When he was still a homicide cop in Bellevue?"

"Yes."

"How did you help him?"

"He called me a confidential informant."

"Detective Gleason said that you solved the case yourself. That's very impressive," she said smiling, as though she meant it.

"Not so impressive. The effort backfired on Jack and me."

"In what way?"

"We both lost our jobs."

"That's unbelievable."

"What's unbelievable is Detective Gleason's role in the incident. You might want to ask him about it, but I doubt you'll get the whole story."

Miller sipped some water. When she set the bottle on her desk, she eyed me carefully. "You don't like Detective Gleason very much, do you?"

"I don't like some of the things he does. He's not an honorable man."

"And Jack Doyle—do you think he's honorable?"

"He has personal issues to deal with, but yes, I believe he is an honorable man."

"Let's talk about his P.I. business. Marie Talbot contacted him because she believed she was the target of a stalker, isn't that right?"

I nodded.

"But she had already signed an agreement with another private investigator, a Mr. Arnold DuPont."

"That's correct."

"Don't you find that strange?"

"Not particularly."

"Would it surprise you to learn that she hired Mr. DuPont for a matter totally unrelated to stalking?"

"No. I don't know why Marie hired Mr. DuPont."

"Mr. Doyle arranged to have a preliminary meeting with Miss Talbot at Java Joe's. You've stated that you have your own business, a concierge service that keeps you quite busy. And yet, you agreed to drop everything and meet with Mr. Doyle and Miss Talbot. Why?"

"Marie was an engineering student at U-Dub. She told Jack that she was about to lose her scholarship. Since I have an engineering degree and many years of work experience in the field, he thought I could help Marie bring her grades up."

"How did tutoring Miss Talbot relate to her stalking case?"

"Jack thought that if I offered to help Marie with her studies it might convince her to sign up as his client."

"I see," she said. But her confused expression told me she did not see. She probably thought that the plan was as far-fetched as I did when Jack proposed the idea.

"Is it correct that you were on your way to the meeting when Miss Talbot fell from the roof of Mr. Doyle's apartment building?"

"Yes. She landed on the sidewalk right in front of me."

"That must have been quite a shock. Did Mr. Doyle come to your aid?"

"Yes."

"But he wasn't at Java Joe's, was he? He didn't run out of the coffee shop along with the other customers. He ran out of his own apartment building."

"I didn't see which direction he came from. I was too upset at the time to notice anything but the bloody body in front of me."

"Why was Mr. Doyle in his apartment instead of Java Joe's?"

"He said that he was delayed by a phone call."

"Do you know who called him?

"No."

"Hmm," Miller said as she flipped through a folder on her desk. She removed a sheet of paper and ran her finger down the page until she found what she was looking for. "According to Mr. Doyle's phone records, the phone call that supposedly caused him to be so late lasted only *ten seconds.*"

She waited for me to respond, but she hadn't asked a question.

"Let me ask you this: were Mr. Doyle and Miss Talbot having an affair?"

"He says not."

She leaned forward and looked me squarely in the eye. "What do *you* say?"

"I say it's highly unlikely."

"But not impossible."

"No."

"Did you know that Marie was pregnant at the time of her death?"

"Not at the time, but I know now."

"We think Mr. Doyle is the baby's father."

"That sounds like a rush to judgment. Have you considered any other persons of interest besides Jack? For instance, Mr. Arnold Dupont?"

"As a matter of fact, we did consider Mr. Dupont. He willingly took the DNA test. Why do you think Mr. Doyle refused?"

"I don't know. You'll have to ask him." I'd had enough of her innuendos and made a show of checking my watch. "How much longer will this take? I have a business meeting to attend in Bellevue that I can't miss."

"I'm sorry to have kept you so long. You've been very helpful, Ms. Ryan. I just have a couple more questions before you go. Did you know that the so-called preliminary meeting at Java Joe's wasn't where Mr. Doyle and Miss Talbot usually met?"

"What do you mean?"

"We have a reliable witness who saw them together at Mr. Doyle's apartment building on several occasions prior to her death. So, I ask you Ms. Ryan, how many *meetings* does it take to hire a private investigator?"

CHAPTER SIXTEEN

JACK

I had a sleepless night. I couldn't stop thinking about Kate and how I'd screwed up. I *had* to convince her that I didn't have an affair with Marie Talbot, let alone father her baby. The first step was to take the DNA test. The second step was to share everything that I knew about Marie Talbot. Third, Kate and I needed to develop a plan of action going forward. As soon as I'd had some coffee, showered and dressed, I headed into SPD headquarters to take the DNA test.

Gleason tried to get me to answer some more questions while I was there, but I politely declined. "I've already answered your questions and have given a sample of my DNA. If you have enough evidence to charge me with a crime, then do so. If not, I have nothing more to say." Gleason couldn't let me have the last word. "Count on it, Doyle. It's just a matter of time before we have plenty of evidence to charge you with a crime—murder in the first degree." I suppose he thought his threat would ruin the rest of my day. It didn't. It only made me more determined to prove him wrong.

I came home and had some more coffee while I jotted down some notes about the case. I started by listing all the persons we'd interviewed and their relationship to Marie. It was a depressingly short list:

Alicia Gonzales – Roommate
Rod Dutton – Ex-boyfriend
Dirk Trstenjak – Half-brother
Scott Patterson –Classmate

A knock at the door interrupted my thoughts. Since I wasn't expecting anyone and rarely had visitors, I looked through the peephole as a precaution. When I saw who stood on the other side, I couldn't get the door opened fast enough. "Kate, I'm so glad you're here."

This was only the second time she'd set foot in my apartment. It's a small one-bedroom unit with just the basics—living room, kitchen, and dining alcove— furnished simply with a couch, coffee table, floor lamp, bookcase stuffed with mostly paperbacks, a comfy recliner, and an area rug to cover the fake hardwood flooring. I don't own a TV. The décor was non-existent except for a framed family photo of Kate, Erin and me. It was taken when we were still together as a family. Every time I look at it, I'm convinced that we will all be together again. Kate was a neat freak and liked a clean, uncluttered house. After our split I'd followed her example and was confident that Kate would think my place passable. But she was in no mood to note how the apartment looked.

"If you really are glad to see me," she snapped, "then you will answer *all* my questions. And you better answer completely. That means no half-truths, omissions or smoke screens. It's called honesty, Jack. But if you continue to keep things from me, you will have to solve Marie's murder on your own." Kate very rarely got angry, but when she did, you knew she meant business. I took her strongly worded ultimatum seriously. But she does look cute when she's riled up.

"Of course, Kate. I want to clear up any questions you have. I take it you met with Gleason and Miller."

"Just Miller. Gleason made sure that I knew he had something more important to do. I think his new partner may be realizing how self-aggrandizing he can be."

"Give her time and she will realize that he's a back-stabber—especially a partner's back. No one stands in the way of Kevin Gleason's ambition. We should warn her."

"Well, right now you need to tell me why your anonymous phone call only lasted ten seconds. You had ample time to get to Java Joe's on time for our meeting."

"I thought it was longer than a few seconds, but I suppose Miller had my phone records."

"Yes, she did. So, just exactly what were you doing that caused the delay, if it wasn't the phone call?"

"I should have known they'd make a big deal out of this. They think the delay was because I was busy shoving Marie off the roof. But Kate, there is nothing suspicious about why I was late. It's just embarrassing."

"Then for God's sake, Jack, tell me what you were doing!"

"Okay, okay," I said. "I was dressed and ready for the meeting when I decided I had time to make some breakfast. I fixed a stack of pancakes with maple syrup and drank a cup of coffee. It was after I'd finished eating that I got the phone call. By the way, I now know who called. I'd like to talk to you about that later."

"Fine. Please continue."

"When I hung up, I got in the elevator and came down to the lobby. Tom, who was on duty, handed me a notice that my mailbox was full. I tend not to check it regularly because it's mostly bills." I could see Kate was getting impatient by the way she was tapping her foot. "It was then that Tom laughed and pointed at my tie. I should have known not to eat in my good clothes."

Kate actually smiled. "Let me guess, you spilled breakfast on your tie."

"Maple syrup, to be exact. I rushed back to my apartment to change but I couldn't find my other tie. I only have two good ones. I finally found it in the laundry basket. How it wound up there I do not know. It was a little wrinkled but unstained, so I set up the ironing board and pressed the tie as best I could. By that time, I knew that I would be late. I rode the elevator to the lobby again and rushed out the door. That's when I discovered a crowd milling around outside the building. One of the looky-loos told me that someone had fallen off the roof. When I spotted you in the crowd, I rushed right over. You know the rest."

"Hmm," Kate said. "That's an interesting story but I doubt Gleason and Miller will buy it."

"Tom can confirm that's what happened, and the timeline will match."

"Why didn't you tell Gleason this when he asked?"

I shrugged. "Gleason thinks I'm a slob and I was embarrassed to prove him right in front of Lucy Miller."

"Oh, please. The half-truth has caused more trouble for you than a little embarrassment would have."

"I shrugged again. "At least I know who called."

"Who?"

"Marie's half-brother." I summarized my conversation with Dirk Trstenjak at the End Zone. He's the only person so far who has had anything negative to say about Marie."

"It sounds like he is still harboring a grudge from when they were kids. But does that make him her stalker? Or her killer? What's his motive? Revenge?"

That's the problem with her ex-boyfriend, Rod Dutton. He spoke highly of Marie, but I question whether it was just an act. He teared up when he talked about Marie and even said a prayer for her. She used to volunteer with him at the local food bank. Did he stalk and kill her because she dumped him?

"And then there's her roommate, Alicia," Kate said. "Why would she kill the person who turned her life around and paid for their luxurious lifestyle? Seems unlikely. I think we can cross her off our list of suspects."

"I agree. We'd be better off trying to find out who her sugar daddy was. My bet is on Arnold DuPont. He's rich enough to fund her lifestyle. Let's say he was in love with Marie but then she got pregnant. Maybe he was afraid that if his affair with a young woman who was also his client became public, his marriage, career, and reputation would be ruined. Sounds like a plausible explanation and motive for murder."

"At least it's more compelling than any reason that her ex-boyfriend, or half-brother would have to kill her," Kate said.

"We could be missing any number of other suspects, but Arnold DuPont should be our focus right now."

"It would be helpful to find out why Marie hired him. Was it for stalking or some other reason? How long were they seeing each other?" Kate paused and stared at me closely. "Which reminds me," she said. "How many times did *you* meet with Marie?"

"Just once before we were to meet with you at Java Joe's."

"I see," she said, frowning. Voice raised, she asked, "Then why did a reliable witness claim that you and Marie were seen together, not just *once*, but on several occasions? At *your* apartment!" She glared at me and hissed, "Is that your idea of full disclosure, Jack?"

I held my hands up in surrender. "No, Kate, but I can explain."

"Please do." Kate had been sitting on the couch, but she now stood by the front door as if she would bolt at any minute.

"Sit down, Kate. This may take a while. The first time I met Marie was at Java Joe's. That's when she told me she had a stalker and wanted to hire a private investigator. I assured her that if she hired me, I would find out who the stalker was and put a stop to it. I explained that there are three stages of stalking: attraction, obsession, and destruction. At that point, I figured it was just some guy from the university who was attracted to her and didn't understand the concept of boundaries. I needed to stop whoever it was before he'd reached the obsessive or destructive stage. She asked what my services would cost, and I offered her a student discount. I had a representation agreement with me, but she said she wanted time to think about it before signing."

"A few days later, she showed up unannounced at my apartment building. I came down to the lobby and we walked to Java Joe's. I thought she had decided to hire me."

"But she didn't hire you."

I shook my head. "It seemed that she just wanted to talk. She said she wanted to get to know me first and asked about my background. I gave her a short pitch that emphasized my years as a homicide detective. But she wasn't interested in my career path and peppered me with a lot of personal questions."

"Like what?"

"Like was I married, did I have children, what were my interests and hobbies, did I play any sports, how long had I lived in Seattle--things like that."

"What did your personal life have to do with hiring you as a P.I.?"

"It didn't. I tried to steer our conversation back to her stalking case, but she cut the meeting short and said that she would be in touch. I'd begun to wonder if she really did have a stalker or if there was something else going on in her life."

When a week went by without hearing from her, I assumed she'd decided not to hire me. So, I was surprised when she showed up at my building again. Once again, I took her to Java Joe's to talk about the case. This time she was distraught and cried. I bought her a latté and she calmed down a little. She said that when the stalking first started, she wasn't too concerned. Lots of guys were attracted to her and she thought it was just a persistent suitor. She'd remembered what I'd said about the three stages of stalking and had decided that her stalker wasn't just attracted to her but was obsessed with her.

I told her that if that were the case, then she shouldn't wait any longer to hire me. I handed her the representation agreement and a pen, but she asked if she could take the document home to read it before signing. Her request didn't make sense to me. If she was as worried as she claimed, she should've been eager to sign it right away. Besides, the agreement wasn't some lengthy document written in complicated legalese that would take a long time to read. Nevertheless, she left with the agreement unsigned."

"That is so strange. It seems like she really didn't want to hire you and was just stringing you along."

"I'd come to the same conclusion. When she showed up at my apartment yet another time, I told her I couldn't take her case. She started crying and begged me to help her. She still hadn't signed the agreement. At Java Joe's she told me that she was about to lose her engineering scholarship. That problem, combined with the stalking, had unnerved her so much she didn't know what to do. That's when I thought of you and suggested that you might be able to help her with her studies while I worked to find her stalker. She had agreed to meet you and I set up the meeting at Java Joe's. We both know what happened next."

"Why didn't you tell me all this in the beginning?"

"I felt responsible for her murder."

"How so?"

"Her stalker had reached the destruction stage and I missed it. I should have assumed that Marie was in grave danger when she first contacted me. If I had, I would've tried harder to get her to sign the agreement. If she'd hired me, maybe she wouldn't have been killed."

"Oh, Jack. You can't blame yourself for her murder. Something about this whole episode seems off to me."

"What do you mean?"

"Four reasons: One, we don't know if she was killed by a stalker; it could have just as easily been someone else. Two, if she had been so scared of a stalker, why didn't she hire you right away? Three, why was she so interested in your personal life rather than in your expertise as a private investigator? And four, why did she lie about her academic ability? I confirmed with an engineering professor of mine who is now the department head that Marie was an excellent student and her scholarship was not on the line. We need to get more information about Marie if we're going to find her killer."

"We?"

Kate smiled. "Yes, Jack, I'm still in the hunt."

CHAPTER SEVENTEEN

KATE

The engineering department at the university organized a memorial for Marie Talbot a week after her death. It was held at Red Square, a large open area on the University of Washington campus. The site, officially named Central Plaza, is paved with red brick and was constructed in 1969. The square serves as the hub for two of the major axes connecting the campus. It is presumably referred to as Red Square because of the color of the red brick surface. Some students, my daughter included, claim that the name originated during an era of student activism in the 1960s and refers to Moscow's Red Square. The jury is still out on that explanation.

Jack and I drove to the memorial together. Jack convinced me that parking would be easier to find if we only used one vehicle. He was right because—even though we arrived early—the available visitor parking was already limited, and it took us quite a while to find a vacant spot. Danielle had called to ask if I would meet her at the memorial. Marie's family would be attending the service and Danielle didn't want to "rub elbows" with her ex-husband's relatives. We agreed to meet at the entrance to Suzzallo Library. Jack and I arrived first and Danielle joined us a few minutes later. She wore a stunning black dress accented with a colorful green scarf and comfortable looking black shoes. It was the first time Jack had seen her since her transformative weight loss. I don't think he recognized her until she greeted us in her unmistakable Texas twang. "So pleased that ya'll came. Sad day, ain't it?" She gave me a big hug and surprised Jack with a hug, too.

"We're so sorry about the circumstances," I said.

"I hear ya, but look how many came to celebrate her life," Danielle said, her eyes roaming the large crowd that had assembled on the square. A cross-section of students and faculty was represented, along with what appeared to be a contingent of worshipers from the church Marie attended. Some gathered in small groups while others stood silently waiting for the ceremony to begin. A makeshift dais and rostrum had been erected on the north side of the square. An enlarged photograph of Marie had been mounted on a tripod alongside a wreath of yellow roses. Several bouquets of mixed flowers also decorated the makeshift stage.

"The huge turnout—especially during summer term—acknowledges how well-liked and special Marie was," Jack said.

"Yes," I concurred. She touched many lives for the good."

Danielle's eyes welled with tears which she quickly wiped with a tissue. "That she did. May God bless her soul."

Jack and I had agreed beforehand that he would mingle with the crowd before the ceremony began while I stayed with Danielle. He hoped to talk to as many students and other attendees as he could to learn more about Marie and her associates. I was to do the same talking to Danielle. "Ladies," he said, "if you'll excuse me, I'm going to wander a bit."

As Danielle watched Jack leave, she said, "He's working her case, ain't he?"

"Well, sort of. As a P.I., he can't compel people to talk to him like he did when he was a homicide detective. Nor does he have access to all the information and evidence that the police have."

"I wouldn't worry about Jack. He has his ways. Besides, it don't take a detective to spot a goat in a flock of sheep."

I chuckled. "I guess that's why he's enlisted me to help him."

"What have you learned?"

"Not much, actually." I gestured to the crowd. "Everyone we've talked to so far has had nothing but praise for Marie. No one can believe that someone would have a reason to kill her."

"Have you talked to her brother, Dirk? I can't imagine he sung Marie's praises."

"Jack met with him and you're right. Dirk said he hated Marie. He could've been her stalker, but why would he murder her?"

"That boy don't need a reason. He's just flat-out jealous of Marie. Dirk thinks she turned his father against him. Maybe he was out for revenge."

"Possibly, but the police think Jack is their prime suspect."

"What? How in tarnation did they come up with that idea?"

"I'm not sure if you know this, but Marie was pregnant at the time of her death."

"I'd heard that but what does that have to do with Jack?"

"The police think Jack was having an affair with her and didn't want the baby."

"So, he pushed her off the roof of his own building? That's crazy."

"Remember Detective Kevin Gleason, Jack's partner in Bellevue? He works for the Seattle P.D. now and is the lead detective on Marie's case. He had a role in Jack's career-ending problems with the Bellevue P.D. Now that he works for the Seattle P.D., he is bound and determined to pin her murder on him."

Danielle shook her head. "I remember Gleason. He's an idiot in search of a village. Jack may be rough around the edges and has some personal issues but having an affair with someone as young as Marie ain't one of them. As for murder? Hell, no. What can I do to help, Kate?"

"Any help you can give us would be appreciated. I do have some questions for you."

Danielle consulted the clock function on her Fitbit. "We have a little time before the ceremony starts. Ask away."

"We know that Marie had been attending college on a scholarship and you told me that her family was financially strapped. Yet, Marie and her roommate were living in an expensive condo with high-end modern furnishings in Redmond. She also wore designer clothes and had accessories that were out of range for most women, let alone a scholarship recipient. For a college student she sure had a classy lifestyle. Were you helping her out?"

"I'd take her out to lunch occasionally, but she never asked me for financial support and I never offered. I did notice that she seemed to have a pretty fancy wardrobe, though."

"Marie's roommate suspects that she had a sugar daddy. Did she ever mention that she was seeing someone special?"

"She told me that she'd broken up with her long-time boyfriend from high school, but she never talked about anyone else in her life. I know that she dated but was primarily focused on school and her volunteer activities."

"Do you think she could have had a relationship with an older, wealthy man?"

"With her good looks and smarts, I'm sure she attracted the attention of a lot of men. But as far as hooking up with a sugar daddy goes, I'm not so sure. Where would she meet someone like that at college? A professor? I wouldn't think a professor would be rich enough. She volunteered at a food bank, which certainly doesn't seem like the place to meet anyone wealthy."

"One of the people we interviewed suggested that she might have met someone at the mega-church she attended in Redmond. What do you think?"

"Possibly. She was certainly gung-ho about the church and its Pastor Bob." The church had several outreach programs that Marie believed in. She told me that she took part in several anti-abortion protests at Planned Parenthood that the church sponsored."

A man stepped up to the lectern and tapped on the microphone. He introduced himself as the head of the engineering department—Professor Cameron Whitworth—and welcomed everyone to the celebration of Marie's life. He recognized some of the college officials that were present and gave a special greeting to Marie's parents. Danielle said Marie's body had been released and her parents would be taking her back to Yakima for a private burial.

Professor Whitworth then introduced Pastor Bob Landers from the Holy Fellowship Church. "Pastor Bob was Marie's pastor and we've invited him to give an opening prayer."

The memorial/celebration of life proceeded with student and faculty speakers telling stories about Marie's life and college experiences. It was inspirational and, at times, humorous. The speakers were followed by a woman from the Holy Fellowship who sang Marie's favorite hymn, "Amazing Grace." Pastor Bob concluded the ceremony with a prayer.

As the crowd began to disperse, I spotted my accountant, Richard Wycoff. "Excuse me, Danielle, I need to speak to someone. I'll be right back."

Richard was talking to an attractive young woman when I approached. "Richard," I said. "Could you spare a minute?"

"Kate! I'm so pleased to see you but sorry about the circumstances." He introduced the woman who seemed irritated that I'd interrupted their conversation. She nodded to me curtly and quickly excused herself. "I'll talk to you tomorrow, Richard."

"I didn't expect to see you here," I said. "How do you know Pastor Bob?"

"The Holy Fellowship is a client. I've been the church's accountant for several years now."

"Did you know Marie Talbot?"

"Not really. I had seen her around when I met with Pastor Bob at the church. She was hard to miss." He shook his head sorrowfully. "Such a waste of a vibrant young woman with her whole life ahead of her."

"It is very sad," I said. "Tell me, Richard, do you know if she was dating anyone from the Holy Fellowship?"

"Why do you ask?"

"I'm helping a P.I. investigate her murder.'

"I thought the police were handling the investigation."

"They are, but the P.I., Jack Doyle, used to be a homicide detective and believes he could be of assistance." I didn't mention that he was my ex-husband and a prime suspect in the case. We've heard that Marie had someone bankrolling her expensive lifestyle. I just wondered if the person could be someone from the church?"

"You'd have to ask Pastor Bob about that. I deal mostly with him and the church treasurer." I'm also on the Board of Directors, but I don't get involved with the parishioners in any meaningful way."

"Who is the church treasurer?"

"Her name is Helen Benton, but she goes by the nickname, 'Sassy.'"

"Does the nickname reflect her personality?"

Richard laughed. "Not at all. She's a fine woman in her sixties with a flair for numbers." He checked his watch. "I have to get back to the office."

"I won't keep you then. If you see or hear anything when you're at the church that might help our investigation, could you call me?"

"Certainly." He caught me off guard when he wrapped his arms around me in a tight bear hug. His face was so close to mine that I inhaled his fragrant aftershave. I didn't know what it was called, but it certainly beat Jack's Old Spice. As I looked over his shoulder, I saw Jack heading our way. Still embracing me, Richard said, "If I hear or see anything, you will be the first person I call. The drink offer is still on the table."

I pulled away from Richard just as Jack approached. He looked at Richard and frowned. "Hope I'm not interrupting anything," he said.

"Not at all," Richard said, smiling at Jack. "I was just leaving. Take care, Kate. Call me when you want to get together for that drink."

"Who was that?" asked Jack.

"Richard Wycoff, my accountant."

"Are you dating?"

"Certainly not. Our relationship is strictly professional."

"Hmm. I don't know much about the professional world, but that hug looked more personal than professional."

"Oh, stop it, Jack," I said, exasperated. The Holy Fellowship happens to be his client."

"I heard some grumbling today about the church. Its ultra-conservative beliefs on social issues don't play well with a certain element at a liberal college."

"Anything specific?" I asked.

"Just that Pastor Bob is supposedly well-known for his anti-abortion stand."

"According to Danielle, Marie was quite active in the church's pro-life movement. She was a regular at the church's anti-abortion protests at Planned Parenthood.

"Hmm, that's interesting. Maybe she ticked off someone who was opposed to her beliefs," suggested Jack.

"Sounds to me like you're grasping at straws now."

"Maybe so, but it could just be the straw that breaks the camel's back."

CHAPTER EIGHTEEN

JACK

The phone call came at six o'clock in the morning. Not my best time of day. Half-asleep and beyond groggy, I fumbled around until I grabbed what I thought was the offending noise maker atop the nightstand. When the alarm clock wouldn't turn off, I threw it across the room. Finally, my brain kicked in and I picked up the phone. "WHAT?"

"Uh, s-sorry, Mr. Doyle. The p-police are on their way up."

"Shit!" I rolled out of bed and rummaged through the clothes I'd tossed on the floor last night. I stepped into some trousers and slipped on my loafers. My tee shirt was wrinkled from sleeping in it but would have to do.

The knock at the door was loud enough to wake the dead, or at least the entire building. "POLICE! OPEN UP!"

When I opened the door, Detective Gleason looked at me with a face that could sour milk. "Let us in, Jack," he demanded.

"Not without a search—"

"Warrant," Gleason said, thrusting the official notice in my hand.

I stepped aside as Gleason, Miller, and a couple of their lackeys entered. "Go for it," I said. "I have nothing to hide."

Gleason flashed me a wicked grin. "We'll see about that." He surveyed the room briefly and then pointed to the kitchen. "You start in there," he told Miller. "I've got the bedroom." The lackeys were ordered to search the living room. "Be sure you check the inside of those books," he said gesturing to the bookcase. He smirked triumphantly, "Jack Doyle thinks he's a clever one, but I know his tricks."

I wadded up the search warrant and threw it in the kitchen trash. "I need some coffee," I said to Miller. "You mind if I make a pot?" She looked sympathetic when, as I expected, she turned me down. "Sorry, you can watch us search, but you can't interfere."

"Then I'll watch you," I said with a dimpled grin. "I've seen enough of Gleason to last a lifetime."

"I can tell," she said, smiling slightly. "I think the feeling is mutual."

"Oh? So, you feel the same way about your partner."

"Nice try, Doyle. You know very well I meant that's how Detective Gleason feels about you."

"I disagree. Gleason wants to see me all right—behind bars."

Her smile faded. "Really? How perceptive of you." She opened a cupboard door. "Now, you'll have to excuse me. I have work to do."

"Be my guest," I said. I leaned against the dining table and watched her tear apart the contents of the cabinets and

VALERIE WILCOX

fridge. As much as the search annoyed me, watching Lucy Miller at work wasn't a bad way to spend the morning, coffee-deprived or not. She couldn't hold a candle to Kate, but her peaches and cream complexion framed by her dark hair was lovely.

It seemed to me that Detective Miller approached her task half-heartedly. She opened the cupboards and perused the contents with disinterest. If she'd been thorough and followed standard procedure, she would've emptied the coffee can, sugar bowl, cereal boxes, and Bisquick box. I wondered whether she thought the search wasn't justified. Or, perhaps she'd begun to question Gleason's motives regarding his persistent pursuit of me.

The search of my entire apartment took just over half an hour. I hadn't expected it to last that long, given how small my apartment was and how minimal the furnishings, not to mention the lack of incriminating evidence. Yet, Kevin Gleason strutted out of my bedroom brandishing a paper evidence bag and a triumphant grin. "Gotcha," he crowed. "Now you need to turn over your laptop and cell phone."

"You have my phone records," I said. "I can't work without my cell."

"Too bad, Doyle. We need to check your email and texts." He directed Miller to bag my laptop that I'd left on the kitchen counter while he took possession of my phone. It occurred to me then that I'd been foolish to stand around ogling Lucy Miller while Gleason rummaged through my bedroom belongings unattended. Based on experience, I should've known that Gleason was capable of manufacturing evidence. If he'd found anything

139

incriminating in my bedroom, I was certain that he had planted it. On their way out the door, Gleason warned me that I should "not leave town." I took his advice for what it was worth—the prattle of a pompous ass trying to sound important.

I spent the rest of the morning putting my apartment back together. The kitchen had been barely touched but the living room had books strewn about, lamps upended, and couch cushions overturned. The bedroom was a disaster. Gleason had emptied every drawer in the dresser and nightstand. All my clothes were on the closet floor. The bed linens had been stripped and the mattress pulled onto the floor.

When order was restored, I went to Java Joe's to finally get a much-needed cup of coffee. Soon thereafter Moira O'Neill arrived. I'd run into Moira at the memorial for Marie and had asked if she'd meet with me today. She had been the records clerk at the BPD when I worked there, but she was now an admin assistant for Arnold DuPont. Moira and I always had a good relationship. Both her parents were from County Cork, Ireland, which meant she discounted my so-called Irish charms as nothing more than a "wee bit" of blarney.

She was tough but she was cheerful and always eager to share a good Irish joke. Sure enough, as soon as she sat down at my table she said, "Here's one for ya, Jack: *A drunk staggers into a Catholic Church, enters a confessional booth, sits down, but says nothing. The Priest coughs a few times to get his attention, but the drunk continues to sit there. Finally, the Priest pounds three times on the wall. The drunk* mumbles, 'ain't no use knockin', there's no paper on this side either!'"

Even though the joke wasn't all that funny, her laughter was infectious, and it caused the couple at a nearby table to crack up. As soon as she'd ordered her coffee and a large cinnamon roll—Moira was a roly-poly sort who didn't count calories—I asked her about her job at DuPont's agency.

"Oh, it's really exciting," she said. "I love it!"

"What do you do, exactly?"

"Just a little of this and a little of that." She locked her eyes on mine. "I know you didn't ask me here to talk about my job duties, Jack. What's up?"

"The police think I had something to do with Marie's murder." They just conducted a search warrant of my apartment a couple of hours ago."

Moira had just forked a big chunk of cinnamon roll into her mouth. She stopped mid-chew and sputtered, "You've got to be joking! What a load of bollocks!"

"Honest to God. The point is they are wrong, and I need to prove it."

"Is there anything I can do to help?" she said, wiping frosting from her mouth.

"Tell me about your boss, Arnold DuPont."

"Why? Do you think he's involved?"

"I don't know, but circumstantial evidence points to him more than it does me."

"In what way?"

I explained about Marie's lifestyle and the possibility that someone rich was the source of it. "Marie was pregnant at the time of her death. I'd like to know if you think it's possible that DuPont had an affair with Marie and fathered the baby she carried."

Moira laughed. "He is rich. I'll give you that. But have you seen Arnold DuPont? He has a face only a mother would love. A blind mother at that. I doubt that a beauty like Marie would give him the time of day."

"She did hire him."

"True, but DuPont is the best P.I. in Seattle. No offense, Jack."

"None taken. Marie told me that she had a stalker. Is that why she hired DuPont? And if so, why contact me, too?"

"I never heard anything about a stalker. It was a missing person's case."

"Are you sure?"

"Absolutely. I typed up the case file."

"Who was she looking for?"

"That I can't tell you. The name of the person was redacted. DuPont is a bugger about confidentiality."

"Did DuPont locate whoever it was?"

"Yes, and closed the case."

"How did Marie pay for his services? I know DuPont doesn't come cheap."

"I don't handle billing, but you're right. His fees are substantial." Moira smiled. "But that's how he can pay his employees so well. My hourly wage is twice what I made at the BPD, plus great benefits." She pulled a cell phone from her handbag and noted the time. "It's been grand talking to you, Jack, but I have to run, or I'll be late for work."

"I understand. One last question. You said that a romantic relationship between Marie and DuPont was unlikely. But the police had DuPont give a DNA sample. They must think he could have had an affair with Marie which resulted in a baby."

"An affair, maybe. A baby, not possible."

"What do you mean?"

Moira's eyes scanned the coffee shop. Leaning across the table, she whispered, "I'm not supposed to know this, but he had the mumps."

"So?"

"So, Anthony DuPont is sterile."

"How do you know that?

Still whispering, she said, "Mrs. DuPont swept into the office one day obviously upset. She burst into her husband's office unannounced, which is something she never does. When I heard her sobbing, I became curious and, making sure I wasn't seen, I listened at the door. Apparently, they'd been trying to conceive for some time and just got the results back. Mrs. DuPont thought it was her fault, but it turned out that her husband was the problem. The mumps made him sterile. You're the only person I've told, and I'd appreciate it if you'd keep this between you and me."

There goes my best suspect.

CHAPTER NINETEEN

KATE

"Hi, Laura, how're you doing?" It had been a while since I'd checked in with Laura Latimore, my new hire. I like to keep in touch with my employees to keep up to date on how things are working—or not.

"Oh, hi Kate! I didn't know you were coming by today. Is everything okay?"

"Of course. I just thought I'd stop by and say hello. I have a meeting in a few minutes with the facility manager."

"I see." She paused to sign a delivery receipt for the UPS delivery that had just arrived. "Glad you're here. I've been wanting to talk to you."

"You don't have to wait for me to show up. Just call me whenever you have a question or concern."

"It really isn't a question. I don't like to complain but the computer system we have here is crap. Excuse my language."

"I'm not very computer-literate so I wouldn't know about that. Why don't you email me an analysis of what is wrong with the system and offer some possible solutions? Be sure to add your years of experience in I.T. to lend credibility to your analysis. I will add my endorsement and send it to the building manager."

Laura's face lit up. "Yes! I'd be happy to do that."

"I can't promise any changes, but it doesn't hurt to ask. I'll mention it to the manager at today's meeting to expect the analysis."

"Thank you very much, Kate."

"Other than the computer issue, how is everything else working out?"

"Great. I really like it here. I didn't know if I'd fit in at first, but everyone has been very kind and friendly."

"Staff or residents?"

"Both!" She hesitated a moment. "Well, there are a couple of residents who are a bit hard to deal with, but I've figured out how to handle them."

"How's that?"

"I just smile and kiss ass."

I laughed. "Yeah, that sums up concierge duties in a nutshell."

We talked for a few more minutes and then I left for my meeting with the facility manager. Afterward, I headed to Seattle to deliver a power point presentation to the board members of a new condominium in downtown Seattle. If Premier Concierge Services got the contract, it would be the third building we had in Seattle. I'd originally thought my business would primarily be on the eastside of the city—in Bellevue and Redmond—but I must go where the action is. And that is in Seattle proper. I'm not complaining. I'm thrilled by how fast the business is taking off. If it keeps up the pace, I don't know how much time I will have to help Jack. We need to get the Marie Talbot case resolved as soon as possible.

The presentation in Seattle went extremely well and I feel certain that I will get the contract based on the favorable responses from the board members. I'd just left the building when my cell rang. "Hello."

"Hi, Kate. It's Danielle. Have you heard from Jack?"

"Not since the memorial. I've tried to call him but haven't been able to reach him yet. Why?"

"My ex-husband just called me. He said that the police told his sister that an arrest of a suspect in Marie's murder is imminent."

"What? Did he say who the suspect is?"

"No, that's why I'm calling. I think you need to warn Jack."

As soon as we hung up, I tried to call Jack again. And again. No luck. Since I was already in Seattle, I decided to see if he was at home. The security guard, Tom, told me that Jack had a meeting at Java Joe's. "I just sent another woman who was looking for Jack over to Joe's."

"Really? Not a police detective, I hope."

"No, she said she was an old friend."

"Okay. Thanks, Tom. I'll see if Jack is still there. But if he returns in the meantime, please tell him that I need to talk to him."

"Sure thing."

I entered the café and was immediately bombarded by the strong aroma of brewing coffee beans. I'm a tea drinker but I've always liked the pleasant smell of coffee. The café bustled with activity—people talking and laughing, cutlery scraping against plates, bussers clearing tables, WI-FI users keyboarding. The place was crowded, but I spotted Jack embracing a woman. She looked to be about my age and wore a clingy silk dress that showed off sexy curves in all the right places. It was a long hug. I'm not the jealous type, certainly not when it comes to Jack. But, to my surprise, my heart felt like it had taken a beating when I saw him with another woman. He was faced my way and when we made eye contact, he immediately withdrew from the embrace. When the woman turned around, she didn't look so sexy. She had dark smudges under her blue eyes and her long blonde hair was stringy and greasy looking. Even so, the woman was very attractive. Jack waved me over to their table with a look that was a cross between guilt and embarrassment. "Kate!" So glad to see you," he said with forced enthusiasm. He gestured to the woman standing next to him. "This is Sally Ann Trstenjak, Marie's mother."

What? Jack knows Marie's mother? Now that I knew who she was, I realized that the haggard and dejected attitude that she projected made total sense. There was nothing sexy about Sally Ann. Just a weary woman who'd tragically lost her daughter to murder. Her grief made my initial jealousy seem petty. "I'm so sorry for your loss," I said.

The words seemed inadequate under the circumstances, but Sally Ann managed a wan smile. "Thank you," she said. Turning to Jack, she added, "I should go now."

"Don't leave on my account," I said.

"My husband is waiting for me in the car. I just wanted to talk to Jack for a few minutes before we left Seattle." She quickly pecked Jack on the cheek. "Please don't contact me," she warned him.

"Wait!" Jack called after her. But she dashed out of the café without looking back. Jack slumped into one of the chairs at the table.

"What was that all about?" I asked, settling into a chair across from Jack.

His face was chalky-white as he rubbed his hands through his hair. "I can't believe it," he said after a moment of awkward silence.

"What's going on? How do you know Sally Ann?"

"You're not going to like this," he said with downcast eyes.

"I'll like it even less if you don't explain what Sally Ann was doing here."

He took a deep breath. "Okay, but don't be mad. I just found out about this a few minutes ago. I had no idea that Marie was . . . oh, hell. I can't say it." Tears formed in his eyes.

Jack's distress touched my heart. I clasped his trembling hands in mine. "Just tell me, Jack," I whispered. My mind was reeling as I tried to comfort him. *Does he know the police are closing in on him? Did Sally Ann tell him he's about to be arrested for Marie's murder? Why didn't she slug him instead of hugging him? Nothing about the scene I'd witnessed made sense.*

Jack shook his head. "I can't, Katie. It just doesn't seem possible. Marie did have a stalker, but that wasn't the primary reason that she came to see me."

I didn't say anything to interrupt, now that he'd begun talking.

"Sally Ann and I knew each other a long time ago, only her last name was Olsen back then. I haven't seen her in years and had no idea Marie was her daughter or . . ." He didn't look at me when he dropped the bomb. ". . . that she's my daughter, too."

I yanked my hand from his and pitched backward as if he'd struck me. "What?"

"It's a shock to me, too."

Shock was an understatement. I was speechless.

"The police shared my DNA results with Sally Ann. I *am* Marie's father. Sally Ann never wanted Marie to know about me, but she was determined to find her "real" father. That's why she hired Arnold DuPont. I'll never know if she would have told me herself. Her reluctance to sign my representation agreement makes sense now. I think she delayed so that she could have more time to get to know me. That explains all the personal questions she asked."

"But . . . when were you and Sally Ann together? Did you cheat on me, Jack?" I felt my face flush and a fiery anger rise inside me.

Jack quickly shook his head. "No, no, Katie. I would never and have never cheated on you. I met Sally Ann when we were separated. You know, that period prior to our divorce."

"We were still married, though. You did cheat on me!"

"*Technically* still married, Katie. I was devastated when you kicked me out. Sally Ann was just a rebound thing. I never loved her. You have to believe me, Kate, you are the only woman I've ever loved."

I pushed my chair back and stood. My anger had reached the boiling point and I had to leave before I said anything I'd regret. "That line is getting old, Jack." I grabbed my handbag and flung the strap over my shoulder. "Sally Ann's warning goes for me, too. Don't contact me!"

CHAPTER TWENTY

JACK

If I ever wanted to drink, it was now. No, that's not right. If I ever *needed* to drink, it was now. But I couldn't get up from my chair. Forget alcohol. Forget even coffee. I was so overwhelmed by the lousy turn my life had taken that I could hardly breathe. The unexpected events of today kept running through my brain on a continuous loop. I hadn't noticed Sally Ann when she first entered the coffee shop. I hadn't even recognized who she was until she sat down at my table.

"Hello, Jack," she said.

I looked at this disheveled woman facing me and wondered why she knew my name. "Excuse me. Have we met?"

She laughed, but it was without humor. A bitter guffaw that caught me off guard. "Oh, yes. You could say we've met."

I looked at her more carefully. She seemed familiar but I still couldn't place her. She was a blonde with blue eyes who would've been quite beautiful if it weren't for the beat-up-by-life vibe that she presented. She wore heavy makeup, but it couldn't conceal the deep wrinkles that lined her face. Her long hair was unkempt and greasy. Most striking of all was the air of sadness she wore like a badge. "I'm sorry," I said. "I can't recall how we know each other."

"Then let me refresh your memory. It was the summer of 2001. The horror of 911 hadn't happened yet and we were young and happy. Well, I was happy. You'd just broken up with your wife. We got to talking over a couple of drinks at Murphy's Pub and things just developed from there. Ring any bells yet?"

"Sally Ann Olsen?"

"It's Sally Ann Trstenjak now."

"Oh my God! Of course. I never made the connection between you and Marie, although I thought she looked familiar. The different names threw me off, I guess. Anyway, I'm so sorry about what happened to her. She was such a lovely young woman. I was at her memorial, but I didn't see you. There were so many people that I couldn't make it to where you were seated and I--"

"Save your apologies, Jack. That's not why I'm here."

I eyed her warily and waited for an explanation.

"I wanted to let you know why Marie sought you out. She was looking for her birth father."

"And I'm a P.I. But she didn't say anything about a birth father. She said she had a stalker."

"Maybe she did. I don't know. But the first P.I. she hired was to locate a missing person."

"I'd heard that."

"I guess you didn't hear the rest of the story. Marie was looking for you and the P.I. she hired was successful."

"But I wasn't missing." And then it dawned. "Wait a minute, are you saying that—"

"Yes, Jack. Marie is your daughter."

"Are you sure?"

"Jesus! What kind of question is that? Of course, I'm sure. Check with the police if you don't believe me. The DNA sample that they took from you proves it."

"Why didn't you ever tell me?"

"Think about it. You and your wife got back together by the time I found out that I was pregnant. I didn't want to be a home wrecker. Besides, by then I'd met Dirk. We got married a year after I had Marie."

I slumped down in my chair. Regret and If Only had gripped me in their claws and wouldn't let go. Regret that I'd lost Kate in the first place. Regret that I'd been so foolish to fall into another woman's arms for comfort. But the biggest regret of all was that I never knew that Marie was my daughter. If only I'd known, I would have supported and loved her just like I've done with Erin. If only she hadn't been killed, we could've had a real relationship. "I don't know what to say, Sally Ann. I'm devastated by the loss."

"I should have told you a long time ago. Maybe I should have told Marie, but I thought it was for the best at the time. She thought her stepfather was her biological father until her half-brother told her otherwise. From then on, her relationship with her stepfather and me was strained. I think that's why she was so eager to change her name and find you. I didn't think she had the money to hire a P.I. so I didn't worry that she'd succeed."

"Apparently, she had a rich benefactor," I said, "but I don't know who it was yet."

"You mean she had a rich lover."

I ran my hand through my hair. "Well, she was pregnant at the time of her death, so I guess lover may be the right word."

"You weren't her lover, were you?"

"For the love of God, NO! But I'm sure as hell going to find out who it was. He was most likely her killer."

"The police told me that they think you killed Marie."

"The police are wrong."

"Well, I wish you luck. I think you're going to need it."

When she stood up, I came around to her side of the table. I asked if I could hug her. "I'm so sorry," I said. "I mean that with all my heart, Sally Ann."

"I know," she said. "I've always known you were a good man."

We were still embracing when I saw Kate walk into the café and it all went downhill from there.

I shuddered at the memory and folded my arms across my chest. Although I was sweaty, my skin felt cold. My stomach was in such turmoil that I thought I'd upchuck at any moment. I must have looked as bad as I felt. A guy at the next table asked, "Hey man, are you okay?" I nodded, but he wasn't convinced. "You look awfully pale and sweaty." He got up and came over to check on me. "I'm an EMT," he said. "Let me feel your pulse."

I tried to wave him off. "No, I'm just—"

He told me to stop talking as he grabbed my wrist. After a moment, he said, "Your heartbeat is weak, and your breathing is irregular. You're in shock, my friend." He pulled his cell phone from his pocket. "I'm calling 9-1-1."

I would've objected, but I felt too weary to even talk. Someone found a blanket and put it over my shoulders. "We need to lower him to the floor and raise his feet," the EMT advised the coffee crowd who'd gathered to watch. The barista helped the EMT lift me off the chair and onto the floor. A woman offered her suitcase-type-purse as a prop for my feet.

"What's going on here?"

The voice sounded familiar, but I couldn't even lift my head to see who had just spoken. I knew people were talking, but it was difficult to understand what was being said.

"He's in shock," explained the EMT. "An ambulance is on the way."

"But we've come to arrest him."

"You'll have to wait. This man needs medical attention immediately."

"Come on, Kevin," said a female-sounding voice. "We can follow him to the hospital."

"No! We can arrest him here first. Then the ambulance can take him."

The EMT must have intervened because the next thing I knew I was lying down in an ambulance. "You'll be okay, buddy," a medic said as he adjusted an oxygen mask over my nose. I don't remember much after that until I arrived at the hospital where an overweight gray-haired nurse in blue scrubs and sensible shoes gave me an I.V. and more oxygen. Sometime later, I had blood and urine tests. My nurse was named Stella and looked like she'd been around the block a few times. She had a Boston or maybe New Jersey accent and exuded a no-nonsense attitude. Street savvy, in other words. Luckily for me, she didn't hold the police in high regard. She told me that two detectives were outside chomping at the bit to be let into my hospital room. "Let them wait," I told her. "I need my rest!" She laughed. "Don't worry, I've got this."

Gleason and Miller were still waiting after my nap when Nurse Stella said that I had another visitor. "You'll want to see her," she said, smiling.

My daughter hurried into the room. She's a beauty just like her mother except with freckles—a natural redhead and eyes as blue as the ocean. "Dad! Nurse Ratched had to fight off two police officers to get me in to see you. What's up with that?"

"I thought you were at the Oregon Coast with Shannon."

"We got back last night. I got a call from the hospital this morning and came right over. What happened? Are you okay?"

"Oh, nothing to get excited about. I had a little shock is all."

"Come on, Dad. The police are outside your door. What have you done now?"

I sighed. "Apparently, I've done *everything* wrong."

Erin plopped into a bedside chair. "Tell me."

I began my sordid tale by explaining about Marie Talbot's death and how her mom and I had teamed up to find out who had killed her. I ended by saying, "The police think I killed her. That's why they're here. They'll arrest me as soon as they can bully their way past Stella."

"What? That's crazy. There must be more that you're not telling me. I called mom, but she refused to talk about you."

"Yeah, that's the worst part of this sad story. She's furious with me because it turns out that Marie was the daughter I never knew I had."

Erin didn't take this news any better than her mother did. She abruptly stood. "A daughter? What the hell, Dad?"

"Sit down, Erin. I can explain."

She didn't sit. "You know I love you, Dad, but this is just too much. Not only do I find out that I have a sister but in the same breath, you tell me that she's been murdered. And the police just happen to think you killed her. I don't think you can *ever* explain this."

I didn't get a chance. She left in a huff. But, unlike Kate and Sally Ann, she didn't tell me not to contact her. I pushed the call button for Nurse Stella. "You can send in the detectives, now," I said.

Gleason tromped into the room with Miller trailing behind him. "I don't know what kind of stunt you're pulling, Doyle, but time is up," Gleason said. He strode over to my bed with an exasperated frown while Miller pulled out handcuffs. "You are under arrest for the murder of Marie Talbot. You have the right to remain—"

"Save your breath, Gleason. I acknowledge the Miranda Warning."

Miller cuffed my hand without the I.V. in it to the bed rail. "As soon as your doctor releases you, we will escort you to the precinct."

Gleason said he'd find the doctor and left.

"How are you feeling?" asked Detective Miller. She seemed genuinely concerned.

"I've had better days."

"If it helps any, I wouldn't worry too much about your arrest. There's a question hanging over the evidence against you."

"What question?"

She looked nervously toward the door and lowered her voice. "Let's just say, there's an internal review in progress."

I'd hoped she'd say more but Gleason returned with a doctor in tow.

Once we arrived at the police station, I was searched, photographed, fingerprinted and relieved of my personal property. All I had on me was an empty wallet, sunglasses and a set of keys to my apartment and auto. The police already had my cell phone. I was then led to a holding cell. The whole process was efficient but demeaning. As expected, I was given no favors as a former cop. If anything, I was treated worse than a criminal by Gleason. He seemed to relish my predicament. Miller, not so much. "Hang in there," she said after Gleason had unceremoniously shoved me into the cell. "I'll be right back."

I didn't know what was up, but Miller's words gave me hope that I'd have a short stay. Lunch and dinner came and went but I couldn't eat the slop that supposedly passed for food. I was still a little nauseous and asked for some Alka-Seltzer, but I got some saltine crackers instead. Two hours later, it looked like I'd read too much into Miller's "I'll be right back" assurance. The cell had two bunks, but I didn't have a cellmate. I suspected that I had Miller to thank for the courtesy. Former cops are not exactly welcomed by other inmates. When another hour went by and Miller still hadn't returned, I resigned myself to spending the night. I'd just stretched out on the lower bunk's thin mattress when Detective Miller returned.

"You're free to go," she said, smiling.

CHAPTER TWENTY-ONE

KATE

"Kate! What a surprise!"

"Hi, Richard. I'm sorry to pop in without an appointment, but Molly said it was okay." I'd walked the six blocks from Java Joe's to Richard Wycoff's office on autopilot. So angry that my eyes filled with tears. At first, I thought the walk would help calm me down. When I realized that I'd walked straight to Richard's office, I decided that I needed to see a friendly face. Jack's revelation about his affair with Sally Ann had upset me more than I thought possible at this stage of our relationship. Although we'd been divorced for many years, the news that he'd had a daughter by another woman was devastating. It didn't matter one iota that we'd been separated at the time.

"No worries. I'm always happy to see you," Richard said. "What can I do for you?"

As usual, he was dressed impeccably in a lightweight summer suit and looked gorgeous. His gracious greeting was just what I needed to hear. Richard was an honest man as well as handsome and refined. "I was just wondering if that invitation for a drink was still open."

He eyed me warily. "Of course. But are you all right? You look a little flushed."

I caught my reflection in an ornately framed mirror behind his desk. He was right. My face was flushed and my eyes puffy. "I just had some disturbing news is all. I'll be okay."

Richard had been stuffing some folders into a leather briefcase when I walked into his office. He set the briefcase aside and came around to my side of the desk. He wrapped his arms around me and held me close. He smelled like he'd just stepped out of a shower. His clean refreshing scent combined with his fragrant aftershave was unexpectedly erotic. I wondered if he could tell how wildly my heart was beating. "I think you need to sit down and have a glass of ice water," he said. "I'll be right back and then we can talk." That he went to fetch the water himself instead of calling for Molly to wait on him was impressive. I think I'd forgotten just how much I'd admired Richard back in the day.

When he returned, he sat in a chair next to mine. "What's going on, Kate?"

"It's a long story," I said. I demurred because I was embarrassed by the whole episode with Jack.

"I'm a good listener."

"I think I'll need something stronger than water to tell you anything."

He grinned and said, "I hear you." He stood and picked up his briefcase. "I was just getting ready to take some financial reports over to the Holy Fellowship Church. I'd be pleased to have you accompany me. We can get that drink afterward at the golf club."

"Oh, no. I don't want to interrupt your schedule. I thought we might meet after you finished working."

"I insist. Didn't you say at the memorial that you wanted to speak to the treasurer at Holy Fellowship? This is your chance."

Did I still want to talk to the treasurer? I'd made it clear to Jack that I was done with him and his murder investigation. I didn't have time to mull it over as Richard took my arm and gently steered me out of the office. What was it about his touch? I felt cared for and special in his presence, but it was more than that. I liked how he made me feel.

"It's a beautiful day for a ride to the Eastside," Richard said. I'll put the top down on the Jag."

He owned a spiffy red coupe that he said was a 2020 Jaguar F-Type. I didn't know what the type signified, but it undoubtedly meant pricey. The ride to Redmond was fun and lifted my spirits immensely. Richard donned a sporty white driving cap and offered me a silk scarf that he pulled from the glove compartment. "I see you come prepared for all your lady friends that you take driving," I teased.

He laughed. "No, actually it belongs to my mother."

Right. But it didn't matter. I was grateful for the scarf, no matter who owned it. Richard was a fast driver and my hair would've been all over the place if I hadn't used it.

I lived in Bellevue, which is right next door to Redmond, but I'd never been by the Holy Fellowship Church. When Richard pulled into the huge parking lot, I was amazed by the structure in front of us. "Wow!" I said. This is a cathedral, not a church." The only building I'd seen that approached that grandeur was the Mormon Temple in Bellevue. The Holy Fellowship was a stain glass wonder with a magnificent gold cross atop a soaring bell tower.

"It is impressive, isn't it?"

"How many people worship here?"

"There are two services on Sunday, and attendance varies. I'd guess there must be at least a thousand or more worshippers in total."

The church was as impressive on the inside as on the outside. "It's a little overwhelming," I said, pausing to take it all in. A sparkling crystal chandelier lit the entry's luxurious black and white marble flooring. An elaborate bouquet of fresh flowers adorned a round polished table next to a padded leather bench. A framed bulletin board on the entry wall was filled with announcements of various church-sponsored events and activities. Beneath the board was a small shelf that held a guest book and pen. The sign above the shelf said, "Welcome Visitors! Please sign our guest book." Richard said I didn't have to sign in. The guest book was for Sunday services and there was always a greeter on hand to welcome newcomers and help them feel at home.

We bypassed the chapel and walked down a short hallway to the treasurer's office. The office was so small and windowless that I wondered how the woman didn't suffer from claustrophobia. No opulence here. There was just room enough for a desk, computer, two chairs, bookcase and file cabinet. The only personal touch was a framed picture on the desk of two little girls—possibly twins--wearing hair ribbons and party dresses.

Richard introduced me to the treasurer who said, "Call me Sassy. Everybody does." She appeared to be in her sixties and was "pleasantly plump" as my mother calls anyone slightly overweight. Sassy had dyed red hair that needed a color update to cover the gray grow-out. She had a winning smile, enhanced by very white teeth—from either a good bleach job or good dentures. But it wasn't her grandmotherly appearance that captured my attention. It was her friendly demeanor that made me feel comfortable in her presence.

Richard handed her the folders from his briefcase. "Here are the records you requested."

"Thanks, dearie." She pulled down her reading glasses perched atop her head. "I'll give them a look-see and get them back to you."

"No rush," Richard said. "And here's a little something extra for you." He took a two-pound box of See's candies from his briefcase and handed it to her.

"See's! My favorite!" Sassy exclaimed, smiling from ear to ear. You're such a sweetheart."

Richard put a finger to his lips. "Shh. Don't tell anyone that. I have an aloof and impersonal CPA reputation to uphold."

Sassy laughed and addressed me, "He forgot to say nerdy."

Richard quickly changed the subject. "Where's Pastor Bob?" he asked.

"He's in the chapel with Lila. There's a wedding rehearsal in progress but it should be about wrapped up now."

"Thanks. I think I'll head on down there. Maybe I can catch Pastor Bob when they're done." He turned and said, "This won't take long, Kate. Want to go with me?"

"She's more than welcome to wait here," Sassy said.

"Thank you, Sassy," I said. "I think I will do just that if you're sure I won't be in the way." I'd have preferred to tag along with Richard but didn't want to interfere with any business he had with the pastor.

"Oh, honey, you won't get in my way." She tapped the white box of candy. "That is, unless you get in front of me and my See's."

After Richard left, she said, "Isn't he the best? Everyone here just adores him." She winked. "Especially the women."

"So, Richard is a member of the Holy Fellowship? I thought he was just the church's CPA."

She opened the candy box. "He's both. And we're pleased to have him. He is so smart and kind."

"I can't argue with that."

She held out the box. "Here take one. Or two. They're really good."

"Umm. How can I resist?" I said, choosing a milk chocolate piece.

Sassy helped herself and set the box down on the desk. Her brown eyes twinkled. as she asked, "Are you dating Richard?"

I smiled and shook my head. "No, I'm a client of his. I have my own business."

"He's quite the catch. If I were a hundred years younger, I'd make a play for him myself."

"Sounds like you care a great deal for Richard."

"Oh, yes, indeed. But he only had eyes for one special girl."

"Had?"

"Marie Talbot. Did you hear about her? She was murdered—pushed off a roof by some monster. It's so sad. Richard took her death very hard. We all did. Marie was a true believer in Christ—smart, beautiful and kind. I was shocked that she was murdered."

"I didn't realize that Richard and Marie even knew each other. He mentioned that he'd seen her at the church but not a word about dating her."

"I'm not surprised. He keeps his personal life personal. But everyone at the Holy Fellowship knew that they were an item." She stuffed a second chocolate in her mouth. "Here," Sassy said, "take another one."

"Uh, thanks, but I need to use the restroom."

She gave me directions and I found it easily. I was stunned by what Sassy had told me about Richard and Marie. I'd used the restroom break as an excuse to take some time to process it. Why hadn't he said anything when he knew that I'd witnessed her fall to her death? I checked my face in the mirror over the sink. I'd become flushed again, but my eyes had lost some of their earlier puffiness. I splashed some water on my face and dried off with one of the conveniently placed hand towels on the counter. I practiced some controlled breathing before leaving. I felt somewhat better but still hurt by deceit. First Jack and now Richard. I didn't know whom I could trust anymore.

I'd just left the restroom when I heard Richard call my name. "Kate, wait up!" A couple walked down the hall alongside Richard. When they reached me, Richard said, "Kate Ryan, I'd like to introduce Pastor Bob Landers and his wife Lila."

Pastor Bob was younger than I expected, late thirties I guessed. He had thinning black hair that he wore long and tied in a loose ponytail at the back of his neck. His trim frame fit well in a three-piece suit that looked even more expensive than Richard's custom-made attire. He wore a Rolex watch and a gold and diamond studded tie clip in the shape of a cross. He wasn't as tall as Richard or as handsome, but his best feature—a broad smile that radiated more wattage than the chandelier in the foyer— diverted attention from his unassuming looks. He seemed more like an ingratiating car salesman than a pious preacher. After we'd exchanged the customary pleased-to-meet-you greetings, Pastor Bob said, "Richard told me that he'd brought you with him today, Kate. He said you were a beauty, but that was an understatement. You, my dear, are dazzling."

His wife, Lila, coughed and shot daggers at the pastor. Lila reminded me of Tammy Faye Bakker, the glamorous televangelist and co-founder of the PTL Club, from some years back. My mother was an avid fan of the PTL and contributed handsomely to the cause. Lila had the same over-bleached blonde hair, pancake make-up, and long lashes coated in mascara. She wore a conservative beige designer dress that she'd accented with lots of flashy bling. Besides the diamond Rolex on her wrist, she wore several gold chains around her neck and rings on almost every finger. The Holy Fellowship must have a generous compensation plan for their pastor and his wife. Maybe it was just the mood I was in, but I took an instant dislike to the couple.

Lila hardly said a word to me, but Pastor Bob was friendly enough for both. I could've done without his attempt to invite me to church services, though. I told him I was happy with my Catholic faith. *No longer practicing, but once a Catholic, always a Catholic.* Pastor Bob dismissed my professed religion as immaterial. "We won't hold your beliefs against you, Kate. We welcome everyone of any faith."

Richard laughed. "Pastor Bob will tow you off to the baptismal font if we stick around any longer." We said our goodbyes and left soon thereafter. Pastor Bob stood at the church entrance and watched us climb into Richard's Jag. His voice carried across the parking lot as if he had a bullhorn. "May God bless you, Kate! Come back anytime."

CHAPTER TWENTY-TWO

JACK

Detective Miller wasn't inclined to give me many details, but the gist of the "problem with the evidence" against me had led to an investigation into Kevin Gleason's actions. He'd been accused of planting a pair of Marie Talbot's panties in my apartment bedroom. "Karma. Ya gotta love it," I said to Miller.

"I thought you were just being a smart ass when you said that I should watch my back around Gleason," Miller said. "But I took your advice anyway. When I discovered that those panties were signed out of the evidence control room in my name, I knew you'd been right to warn me."

Gleason was placed on administrative leave pending the outcome of an internal review. I was free to go while the hunt for Marie's killer continued. She didn't say I was completely off the hook, but she did admit that they didn't have any solid leads. My personal hunt for Marie's killer would continue as well. But I didn't have any solid leads, either. Whether Kate would hunt alongside me was yet to be determined. Based on her comments, the chances were slim to none.

After I'd picked up my belongings from the precinct, I headed home. I was exhausted but too wired to sleep. With nothing else to do, I made a pot of coffee and thought about what I should do next. I hadn't eaten anything all day, so I made a tuna sandwich to go with the coffee. I'd just finished eating when the phone rang.

"Hello."

"Hey, P.I. man. Do you know who this is?"

My anonymous caller was back. "Dirk Trstenjak," I said. What's on your mind this time around?"

"I don't have a cold anymore, so I didn't think you'd recognize my voice. How'd you know it was me?"

"No guessing involved, Dirk. I'm an experienced detective." *Poor but experienced.*

"Are you still investigating Marie's murder?"

"Wherever the leads take me."

"I'm in Yakima right now for her funeral mass. Half the family thinks you're the killer and the other half thinks it's someone from that kooky religion she got mixed up with."

"What do you think? And more important, why do you care? Didn't you tell me that you hated Marie?"

"I don't trust any religious types. Especially rich holier-than-thou types. Marie and I weren't on the best of terms, but I still want justice served."

"Do you have a suspect in mind?"

"No, but I told you before that you should investigate that church. If you haven't, I think you should take my advice now. Maybe you'll find Marie's sugar daddy there.

The Holy Fellow mega church or whatever it's called, is super rich. The church paid for her burial plot and headstone and even sent cash for a catered reception after the funeral mass. Sounds like a guilty conscience to me."

"Or maybe a generous remembrance of a beloved member of their church family."

"That's a crock and you know it. You want to find Marie's killer, then start with the rich holy roller dudes."

It was a viable avenue to explore, especially since there weren't any other avenues on my map right now. I remembered talking at the funeral about going to the church with Kate. Guess that's not going to happen now. I poured a second cup of coffee and opened my laptop. I used to be an altar boy back in the day, but my only experience with church attendance these days is attending St. Charles' yearly spaghetti feed and, occasionally, a fund-raising bingo game that my Aunt Tillie drags me to. I needed to get up to speed on what a mega church is generally and The Holy Fellowship specifically. My daughter claims you can find out about anything on the Internet so that's where I started.

Erin was right. There was almost too much information to process. I skimmed through a few articles until I felt like I was reading the same stuff over and over. Basically, mega churches are those that have a large congregation of 2,000 or more a week. One article talked about a mega church in California that had 8,000 members! Nearly all are found in the suburbs of large cities, which makes sense. Hard to imagine a mega church in rural America that could draw anywhere close to 2,000 worshippers. Apparently, almost one-half of mega churches are nondenominational and have a conservative theological orientation. Those typically attracted to mega churches are generally consumer-oriented, highly mobile, well-educated, middle class, with the median age estimated at thirty-eight years or less. Sounds like a description of Marie Talbot. The main takeaway in all the articles was that mega churches are mega businesses. They are corporations led by a senior minister and an executive board overseeing business affairs. And, like the CEOs of major corporations, the pastors are well compensated. I recognized the name of one well-known preacher who had a net worth of over forty million dollars and a house valued at ten million. A good gig if you could get it.

The next step was to focus on The Holy Fellowship mega church. When I consulted the church's web page—an expertly designed and easy to use site—I found a color photo of a massive structure with a tall bell tower affixed with a gold cross. The photographer captured the edifice with sunlight shining down on it, glowing as if blessed by God himself. The choices for exploring the site were listed at the top of the page and included an About Us section which I figured would give me the most information.

The About Us page had photos of the senior pastor and his wife, Pastor Bob and Lila Landers, and all twelve members of the Board of Directors. Each photo included a brief biography which really didn't tell me much. Most read like the biographies of politicians—all positive spin on backgrounds and impressive accomplishments. I zipped through the section and was about to click on Church History when something made me pause. I backtracked to one of the photos and looked closely at the man named

Richard Wycoff. He sat on the Board of Directors and his day job was Certified Public Accountant in Seattle. It took me a moment to remember where I'd seen him before. Wycoff was the handsome man who I'd caught embracing Kate at the memorial. She said he was just the accountant for Premier Concierge Services, but the way he'd looked at Kate told another side to the story. I re-read his biography which, like the others, was a slick retelling of his educational background, current career, and role in the church. I noted that he'd graduated from the University of Washington the same year Kate did. His passion, besides playing with numbers, was playing golf.

Despite the late hour, I was still not sleepy. Just more wired. All the caffeine had done its job. Discovering the handsome and successful Richard Wycoff involved with The Holy Fellowship (and Kate) ensured that I wouldn't be slipping into bed anytime soon. I clicked on Church History to see what other gems would pop out.

The church was founded in 2000 by Pastor Norman Duncan. He was a charismatic leader who saw the membership grow from a relatively small congregation to over a thousand members in five short years. The historical record didn't say why he left in 2014 but I can understand why that little detail was omitted. I'd forgotten all about the scandal until I saw his name. It seems that the pious pastor who railed against those who participated in the evils of pornography, homosexuality and drugs was an active consumer of the very same sins. Pastor Bob Landers was the youth pastor at the time and assumed the senior pastor role in 2014 when Duncan resigned to "spend more time with his family." Politicians and preachers have so much in common. With Pastor Bob's leadership, the church continued its rapid growth and at present numbered 1,545 members. A little short of 2,000 but enough to launch a funding campaign to enlarge the facility to accommodate the anticipated growth.

Next, I clicked on Activities and Events. There was a long list of social activities offered, from Bible classes to youth programs. Sponsored events in the community that the church endorsed included a lot of volunteer opportunities. A pro-life rally at the local Planned Parenthood facility to protest abortion was a regularly scheduled event. Photos of past protest rallies were included. I took a close look at the participants and was not surprised to see Marie Talbot front and center carrying a large sign that read, "Choose Adoption!" I wondered if adoption was what she'd planned for her baby.

I finally closed my laptop at 3:00 am. I'd gleaned some useful information but what I really needed was a "deep dive" as my daughter calls her searches. Erin is a computer expert at a local tech company now, but she used to be quite the hacker in her day. If I hadn't completely ruined my relationship with her, I needed to talk to her about a deep dive into the Holy Fellowship and its leaders. I wanted to know what they didn't want the public to know. Sounds cynical, but I was a cop for over twenty years. Cynicism goes with the territory.

CHAPTER TWENTY-THREE

KATE

Our ride to the Green Meadows Golf Club took just five minutes. Neither Richard nor I said much but I think he could sense something was bothering me. He parked the car in a vacant spot near the entrance and asked, "Are you okay?"

"I'm fine."

"In my experience, when a woman says she's fine the way you just did, it means she's anything but."

"I'm sure you've had lots of experience with women. Why didn't you tell me that you and Marie Talbot were dating?"

He took off his driving cap and ran his fingers through his hair. "Sassy must have told you that. I thought she might."

"I don't understand why you didn't tell me yourself."

"Mainly because it isn't true."

"What?"

"Let's go inside and I'll tell you everything you want to know over a drink."

I wasn't enthused about having a drink with him anymore but decided I wanted to hear his explanation. Could it be any more startling than Jack's confession?

The 19th Hole was a typical golf club bar but with an added dose of luxurious furnishings. It wasn't as grand as the church we'd just left but it was country club fashionable. Richard asked the hostess to seat us outside on the patio. We sat at a table overlooking a rock waterfall and pond stocked with colorful Koi. "So, what's up, Kate?" he asked after we'd ordered our drinks.

"The question is: what's up with you? You told me at the memorial for Marie that you didn't really know her. Then today Sassy tells me that you not only knew her, but that you were dating her as well."

"Sassy is quite a gossip.

"Gossip usually has a ring of truth to it."

"Quite right. But in this case, we used Sassy's reputation for passing on gossip. You see, we needed to get the word out that I was in a relationship with Marie."

"What are you talking about? Were you or were you not in a relationship with her?"

"No, we weren't dating, but we wanted everyone to think that we were."

"Well, that's certainly a novel explanation. I have no idea what you mean. And for that matter, who is *we*?"

Richard waited until the server delivered our drinks before he continued. "Look," he said, "it's like this. Marie was a beautiful young woman. The problem was that her beauty was attracting too much unwanted attention from would-be suitors. Marie was flattered, but she was more interested in serving Christ than dating anyone. She was very active in community events that were sponsored by the church. The attention was so annoying for her that she went to Pastor Bob for counseling. He's the *we* I referred to."

"Marie told Jack Doyle that she had a stalker. You think it was one of these would-be suitors from The Holy Fellowship?"

"I'm not sure if it got to the point of stalking, but the single guys at the church just wouldn't leave her alone. She didn't want to hurt anyone's feelings, but she couldn't seem to make the guys understand that she wasn't interested in them."

"Only Jesus."

"Exactly. So, Pastor Bob came up with an idea. If everyone at church believed Marie was in a steady relationship, the unwanted attention would stop."

"Let me guess. That's where you came into the plan."

He smiled sheepishly. "Pastor Bob asked me if I would go along with the idea and I agreed. But it was a relationship in name only. Marie and I never dated. We'd sit together at church services but that was just to give the appearance of being together."

"Did Sassy know that your relationship with Marie was a sham?"

"Oh, no. It was crucial that she think we were a couple. We knew she would spread the word. And she did."

"Interesting subterfuge, especially coming from a pastor."

"Pastor Bob is a great guy with an understanding heart. He convinced Marie and me that Jesus would not hold the deception against us."

I didn't know whether to believe Richard or not. It seemed like such a far-fetched plan to avoid potential suitors. If it was such a success, then who was she seeing? Marie had to have been seeing someone since she was pregnant. Was Richard her lover despite his claim? I thought his story over for a few moments while I watched the Koi swimming in the pond. Richard took the opportunity to order us another round of drinks. "Okay," I said. "Let's assume that what you've told me is true. Did this plan also involve funding Marie's elaborate lifestyle?

"What elaborate lifestyle?"

"Come on, Richard. Surely you know that Marie was a kept woman."

"What are you talking about?"

"Marie attended college on a scholarship, but someone footed the bills for a fancy condo in an upscale Redmond neighborhood and a designer wardrobe. You didn't know this?"

He shook his head. "I assumed she came from a wealthy family."

"Did you know that she was pregnant?"

Richard was either a good liar or a good actor, or both. He seemed stunned by this news. "How do you know that?"

"Jack Doyle had to take a DNA test to prove that he wasn't the father of her baby. It turns out, he wasn't her lover. Jack was Marie's *father*."

"Well, that sure puts things in a different light."

"You think?"

"I can't believe it."

"Believe it or not, it's the truth. Looks like her deception went a little further than what you and Pastor Bob concocted."

Our drinks arrived and Richard immediately took a big swig of his. "I'm so confused," he said. "Was Marie's lover the same person who killed her?"

"That's the theory that Jack Doyle is pursuing. He thinks it has to be someone rich who was content to have a secret relationship with Marie but came unglued when she got pregnant."

"And that's why she was killed? Her lover didn't want the baby?"

"Think about it. If her lover was married or had some other reason to keep his relationship with her a secret, a baby would be a major problem."

"And Marie would never consent to an abortion. She was one of the most dedicated pro-life activists in the Holy Fellowship."

"You'd know what her feelings were about abortion better than I would. What about you? Are you opposed to abortion?"

He shrugged his shoulders. "I'm pro-life but I think there are instances when abortion might be the only choice—as in incest, rape or the mother's health risk."

I studied Richard over the rim of my beer glass. "If you didn't have a relationship with Marie, who do you think did? Another wealthy church member?"

Richard shook his head and looked at the waterfall. "I have no idea, Kate. That's the honest to God's truth. All I know is that I'm not the person your Jack Doyle is looking for."

We didn't have much to say after that, so we finished our drinks and left. I got a phone call from Erin just as we were about to get into the car. "I need to take this," I told Richard. "It's my daughter." I moved a foot or so away and answered. "Hi, Erin."

"Mom, I'd really like to talk to you about Dad."

"I told you that I didn't want to discuss him."

"I went to see him at the hospital, and he told me about Marie Talbot."

"He's in the hospital? What happened?"

"Don't worry. He's okay. He had a panic attack or something like that. Anyway, could you come over to my place? I really need to talk to you."

Since we were already in Redmond, I told Richard that he could drop me off at her townhome instead taking me back to Seattle. I think he was relieved to get rid of me. I'm not sure how *I* felt. I liked Richard a lot but the whole situation with him and Marie Talbot was unsettling. *Bizarre* might be a better term when you add Jack to the mix. Maybe it would be good for me to talk to Erin about all this. But I never got the chance until much later.

I had reservations about riding in the car with Richard after he'd been drinking but he assured me that he was well under the limit. I should've listened to the little voice in my head telling me to call an Uber. I don't know if his driving was impaired by the alcohol or whether he was distracted by our earlier conversation or both, but the result was the same. He rear-ended a Volvo in front of us which had stopped suddenly for a yellow light. The Volvo wasn't damaged too badly, and the driver wasn't injured. The Jaguar, however, was not drivable.

Despite his assurances, Richard failed a breathalyzer test and was cited for a DUI. He apologized to me profusely before he was taken into custody. The Jag's air bags deployed as they should, and Richard was uninjured. My chest and head hurt a little, but I thought I was okay. The paramedics thought otherwise and insisted that I let them take me by ambulance to Overlake Hospital. I just wanted to go home.

CHAPTER TWENTY-FOUR

JACK

Five-year-old Shannon answered the door. "Grandpa!" she cried, flinging herself at me. I lifted her up and carried her down the hall of Erin's townhouse. "Hey, Chipmunk, you're getting too big for your old grandpa to carry. I struggled for breath as I set her down in the living room. "You're not a little chipmunk anymore. Have you been eating nuts instead of hiding them like a good little chipmunk?"

Shannon giggled. "Silly Grandpa. You know I love chocolate nuts."

"Well, then, I guess this is for you," I said, handing her a bag of M&M chocolate covered peanuts.

"Look what Grandpa gave me, Mama."

The room's temperature suddenly dropped to iceberg level. I shivered as Erin regarded me with a look that could chill a polar bear to the bone. "Hey," I said. It's just a little candy."

"It's not the candy, Dad. What are you doing here?" Erin wore a bathrobe and held a coffee mug.

The unmistakable aroma of pancakes wafted from the kitchen. I sniffed the air and said, "Are those pancakes I smell?"

"Yes!" shouted Shannon. "Me and grandma made cottage cheese pancakes this morning. Come in the kitchen and sit down. I'll serve you myself." She tugged on my arm to lead me into the kitchen. "Stop," said Erin, raising her hand like a traffic cop. It was too late. Shannon was on a pancake mission.

I hadn't expected to see Kate at Erin's today, but I was glad she was here. She sat at the table in a bathrobe and slippers eating pancakes. She looked up at me and frowned. The kitchen was warm and cozy until Kate's frown. I shivered again. Not because of Kate's chilly reception; it was the cervical collar around her neck and worrisome facial bruises that froze me to the core.

"My God, Kate! What happened?"

She shrugged off my concern. "It looks worse than it is."

Erin helped Shannon scoop a stack of pancakes onto a plate. "Now, you better get your backpack ready. Your dad will be here any minute."

Shannon set the plate in front of me. "Daddy's taking me skating this weekend."

"That sounds like fun," I said. "Say, is there any of that coffee left?"

Erin bristled but poured me a cup. As soon as Shannon scampered off to her bedroom, I asked Kate, "Now, could you please tell me what happened?"

"Mom was in a fender bender," Erin answered, placing a gentle arm around Kate's shoulder. "I went to the hospital and picked her up. She got whiplash and a concussion when the air bag deployed."

"A slight concussion. I'm okay," Kate said. "Erin insisted that I spend the night, but I'll be leaving soon."

"I can give you a ride home," I offered, hopefully.

Kate started to shake her head and winced. "Not necessary. Erin said she'd take me."

"All right. But since we're all here, could we please discuss a few things?"

"Like what?" asked Erin. "We know everything now. You had an affair and fathered another daughter. A daughter who apparently had an affair also. A daughter who wound up murdered. The last time I saw you, the police were waiting outside your hospital door to arrest you for her murder. Have I missed anything?"

The doorbell rang before I could answer Erin's razer-edged summary. I stayed in the kitchen with Kate while Erin and Shannon greeted Rob. I finished eating. Kate silently watched me as she drank her coffee. Shannon ran back into the kitchen to tell us goodbye before she left. "Love you, sweetheart," I said. "Have a good time with your dad."

After Shannon had scurried off, I looked pleadingly at Kate. "I know you and Erin are disappointed, hurt and justifiably angry. But I'd really like to talk everything over with both of you. Could you just give me a few minutes?"

"I think it would take more than a few minutes," Erin said, entering the kitchen.

"Kate?" I implored.

"Fine," she said, sighing. "Let's clear the air. Then maybe we can put this whole painful episode to rest."

We moved into the living room with fresh mugs of coffee. Kate and Erin sat side by side on the couch while I sat across from them in a ladder-back chair that was more comfortable than it looked. I started the discussion. "First, I think you know how much I love you both. And Shannon, too. At least I hope that you know that. I'm not going to justify anything that I've done because there is no excuse for the distress I've caused. All I can say is that I'm sorry and that I hope you can eventually forgive me. I desperately want us to be a loving family again." I caught Kate and Erin exchanging dubious looks. "I know, I know. It's a long shot but I had to say it."

Erin stood. "Okay, you've said it. I think you need to leave now."

"Hold on. I also wanted to tell you that the police no longer suspect me of murder."

"How did that happen?"

I grinned. "Ironically, I have Detective Kevin Gleason to thank for my release from custody."

"What?"

"He was up to his old tricks again. He thought he could seal my fate by planting incriminating evidence against me." I repeated what Detective Miller had told me about the trouble Gleason was in.

"Good," said Kate. "He's been on a never-ending crusade to ruin you. It's time he was stopped."

"That brings me to my next point. Miller said that they don't have any solid leads on another suspect, but the hunt for Marie's killer goes on. I never knew that Marie was my daughter until her death. That's a regret I will take to my grave. I wanted to find her killer before, but now I'm more determined than ever to bring her killer to justice."

Erin was an easy read. She was done with me. I didn't have a fix on Kate's expression, but her next question suggested that she was still interested in the case.

"How are you going to do that?" asked Kate. "Do *you* have any leads?"

"I'm glad you asked that. As a matter of fact, I do. That's why I came here this morning. To apologize to Erin and ask for her help."

Erin's brows shot up. "*My* help? Even if I wanted to and I don't, what can I possibly do?"

"I'll get to that in a moment. Kate, remember when we were at the memorial service and you introduced me to Richard Wycoff?"

"Yes," she said warily. "What about him?"

"I got a phone call yesterday that jogged my memory a bit. I remembered that we had talked about checking out the Holy Fellowship Church that Marie attended."

"What's her church got to do with anything?" asked Erin.

"Jack's working theory is that someone rich was bankrolling Marie's lifestyle. When she got pregnant, the affair turned sour and led to her murder."

"I still don't get it. Why check out her church?"

"The Holy Fellowship is a megachurch that attracts many well-heeled worshipers from Redmond and Bellevue," I said. "It's possible that her benefactor is one of them. No one else seems to fit the role."

"Don't forget Arnold DuPont," Kate said. "He's rich and had a relationship with Marie that could've included an affair."

I slapped my forehead like I was in a V-8 commercial. "That's right!" With all that's been going on, I forgot to tell you. I've ruled DuPont out."

"Why?"

"He can't be the father of Marie's baby." I told them what I'd learned about his sterility from Moira.

"He could still be her benefactor," suggested Erin. "Maybe he killed her because she got pregnant by someone else."

"Good point," I said, pleased that Erin's curiosity had been aroused. Maybe she'd come around after all. "I'll follow up on that. In the meantime, I am hoping that both of you will consider helping me learn more about the Holy Fellowship."

"Here it comes, Mom. I knew he'd try to drag you into his so-called investigation again. And now he's even included me. Talk about hubris."

I wasn't sure what *hubris* meant, but I figured it wasn't something good.

"Actually, Erin, your dad didn't drag me into his investigation. I volunteered to help him."

"You're not seriously thinking about teaming up with him again, are you?"

Erin made it sound like a match made in hell. "I'm not asking your mother to marry me again, just help me learn more about the church and its members. Maybe her CPA could introduce us to Pastor Bob for a start."

"Richard has other things to worry about right now. He got arrested last night."

"What?"

"It's probably in today's newspaper or online. He comes from a prominent Seattle family and his arrest will be big news. Getting a DUI is not a pleasant experience for anyone. For a Wycoff, it's particularly damaging."

"How do you know about the DUI?" I asked.

"Because I was with him at the time."

"Mom! You didn't tell me that part of the story. I thought it was your car that was hit."

"Now you both know. He's texted me twice this morning to see how I'm doing. I never answered."

"You told me that you weren't dating Wycoff," I said. "Who's keeping secrets now?"

"I wasn't dating him. I just rode along with him to the Holy Fellowship so he could deliver some financial statements to the church treasurer."

"I'm confused," Erin said. "You willingly got in a car with someone who'd been drinking?"

"Not my best moment."

"My God, Katie. You could have been killed!"

"But I wasn't, so let's just drop the subject, okay? In any event, I don't have to ask Richard to introduce you to Pastor Bob. Or, his wife for that matter. I met them both while we were at the church."

"And?"

"And I wasn't impressed with either of them. Especially after what Richard told me about Pastor Bob."

This conversation had taken a completely different turn from what I had anticipated. Kate was on a roll, so I asked her to go on.

"Richard's a great CPA. I knew him in college and contacted him when I needed an accountant for Premier Concierge. He's always impressed me as an honest and capable gentleman. "

"I hear a 'but' coming," Erin said.

"Well, sort of. He told me at the memorial that he didn't know Marie Talbot well; he was just the accountant for the church. When I accompanied him to the church and he left to meet with Pastor Bob, I talked to Helen Benton, the church treasurer. Sassy, as she likes to be called, told me that not only did Richard know Marie, they were very much an item."

"Hah!" I said. "Not so honest after all."

"I confronted Richard about his misrepresentation or lie," Kate said, "and he explained why he hadn't told me." Kate then repeated the whole "story" as Richard called it.

I shook my head in disbelief. That is one of the most cockamamie stories I've ever heard. And I've heard plenty as a cop."

Apparently, Erin didn't think much of the "explanation" either. "Let me get this straight," she said. Marie was annoyed by all the unwanted attention she received because it distracted from her service to Jesus?"

"That's what Richard said. Pastor Bob's idea was that if everyone, especially a known gossip like Sassy, knew that Marie and Richard were in a relationship, then she wouldn't be pursued by anyone else."

"Oh, Mom, that's ridiculous. All she had to do was put a ring on her finger and say that she was engaged to someone from out of state. But she must have been seeing someone local because she was pregnant. Unless this is the second virgin birth, I'm nominating Richard Wycoff as the father."

"I second that nomination," I said. "It looks like we need to attend Sunday services at the Holy Fellowship tomorrow. How about it, Katie? Are you willing to go with me?"

Kate and Erin exchanged looks. When her cell phone buzzed, Kate said, "It's another text from Richard. Should I text him back?"

"Yes," said Erin. "Tell him you're going to the Holy Fellowship worship service tomorrow and will talk to him then."

"So, you're okay with me helping your Dad again?"

"I think you need to decide that for yourself, but if I were you, I'd want to find out what's really going on with Richard and that church."

Erin's turnaround was amazing. I grinned and clapped my hands. "Grand! Let's do it, Kate. And Erin, there's something you can do, too.

"I can't believe I'm saying this, but what do you have in mind?"

CHAPTER TWENTY-FIVE

KATE

"Are we late?" I asked, noting all the people streaming out of the church.

"We're fifteen minutes early. Maybe another service just ended."

"No, the nine o'clock service is the first one held on Sunday. The next one isn't until 11:00 o'clock."

"Wow!" Jack exclaimed as he gazed at the church. "The website photograph of the building didn't do justice to the majesty of this place. It looks like an immense cathedral." As his eyes roamed the site, he said, "Something big is going on. Look over there." He pointed to several police cars, a fire truck, and an ambulance on the south side of the parking lot.

"That doesn't look good."

Parking was limited but Jack had found a spot when another car pulled out. "Stay here," he said. "I'll go see if I know any of the officers. Maybe I can find out what's going on."

I didn't like being told to stay put. "This is the Redmond P.D.'s jurisdiction. How would you know anyone?"

Jack hopped out of the car. "I worked on a Bellevue-- Redmond joint task force back in the day," he said, hustling off before I could get out of the car and follow.

An officer had attached yellow caution tape to the entry's massive oak doors so I couldn't go inside the church, either. Lots of people milled about in the lot, apparently wondering what was going on, too. Thinking that I might see Richard in the crowd, I got out of the car to look for him. He'd been released from custody and had agreed to meet me here. Money and a good lawyer do wonders to expedite the bureaucratic process. I was a little embarrassed by the cervical collar I wore, but I figured I needed it. My neck still hurt more than I let on. I downed some Ibuprofen and climbed out of the car. As I meandered through the crowd, looking for Richard, I overheard scattered talk about what had happened. None of it made sense. Someone said there'd been a shooting and hostages were taken. If the church had been the target of a terrorist attack, I'd have expected to see a SWAT team on site.

I didn't see Richard anywhere, but I did spot Sassy standing next to a news van from KING TV. A reporter held a mike in front of her while a cameraman filmed her remarks. As I approached, Sassy was in tears. "I can't believe it," she sobbed. "He was the nicest and most decent man I've ever known." I was afraid that I knew who she was talking about.

"Tell us what happened," the reporter said.

"I found him. I'd come into the office early to get a couple of things done before the worship service started." She dabbed at her eyes with a lace handkerchief. "Oh, it was just awful. He was spread-eagled on the floor with blood pooling around his head."

"Who was he?" asked the reporter, echoing my unspoken question.

"Richard Wycoff, the church's CPA."

The reporter looked surprised but kept a professional attitude. "Are you saying that Richard Wycoff, the prominent Seattle accountant, is dead?"

Sassy broke down crying, uncontrollably. The reporter directed the cameraman to follow her and they left to find another witness or, more likely, to get Sassy's story confirmed by the police. I quickly approached Sassy and put my arm around her shoulders. "I'm so sorry, Sassy," I said. "How can I help?"

She looked at me through red-rimmed eyes, but I don't think she recognized me. "Oh, thank you," she said. "You don't have to . . ." She paused and looked at me more carefully. "I've met you," she said. "You know Richard."

"That's right. I'm Kate Ryan. We shared the chocolates he gave you."

"Did you hear? He's been killed. I just can't get over it."

"Yes, I overheard your conversation with the reporter. I'm so sorry. I liked Richard a lot."

"I wonder how this will affect the investigation," she said.

"Investigation?"

"Goodness me," she said. "I've done it again. I'm not supposed to say anything about what Richard and I were working on. No one knew, not even Pastor Bob."

I couldn't let that go, secret or not. "You can tell me, Sassy. You and Richard were investigating something?"

She whispered in my ear. "There has been some funny business going on with church funds. We were researching the records to see if we could determine who had been accessing the accounts without authorization."

"Did you have anyone in mind?"

"No, but Richard told me we needed to get a computer expert involved. We understood that the funds had been stolen, embezzled or whatever, but the computer trail to trace the source was too complicated."

"Sounds like you need to report this to the police. Have you talked to them yet?"

"Briefly, but just about how I found the body. They told me to wait outside and a detective would contact me to take a formal statement. I guess I can tell the detective about our investigation then."

"Yes, it may be an important avenue for them to pursue in their search for Richard's killer."

Sassy's tearful eyes widened. "Do you think whoever was cheating the church accounts killed Richard?"

"I don't know, but the police need to investigate the possibility."

By this time, several ladies from the church had approached to offer Sassy their comfort so I excused myself. I wandered back to our parked car and discovered Jack sitting inside. It had begun to rain as I climbed into the car. "Learn anything?" I asked him.

"Not really. Where were you?"

"I ran into a woman I'd met the other day. Sassy Benton, the church treasurer. She found Richard Wycoff's blood-stained body in her office."

"Wycoff's dead?"

I nodded. His death had upset me more than I wanted Jack to know. "Shocking, isn't it? And that's not all." I told him about Richard's and Sassy's investigation into the misuse of church funds.

"That's interesting. It's possible that the Church's missing money and Richard's murder is somehow connected to Marie Talbot's murder."

"Are you dismissing Richard as a suspect in her murder?"

"Not necessarily, but I think this is where Erin can be a big help. She's already agreed to do a deep background computer search on Wycoff, Pastor Bob and his wife, and the Board of Directors. She should know how to access complicated accounts to identify the money trail. As the saying goes, "Follow the Money!"

Erin was in her home office when we arrived. She barely noticed us as she typed on the keyboard. Jack and I sat down in matching chairs and didn't speak until she finally looked up. "You're back earlier than I expected," she said. "Did you learn anything useful?"

Jack filled her in on what had happened to Richard Wycoff and what he'd been investigating. "We think that your next avenue for a computer search is the Holy Fellowship's finances. You can be assured that there's where the homicide detectives will have their techies exploring."

"Makes sense. Would you like to hear what I've found out about the so-called preacher and his wife?"

"By all means."

"First, Pastor Bob Landers has a criminal record. It happened when he was just a teenager and the records were sealed. But they're easily accessible if you know what you're doing."

"And you do."

"Of course. He was arrested at sixteen for robbing a convenience store with a firearm."

"Where did this happen?"

"New Jersey. That's where his family is from. He apparently got religion when he was in juvenile detention. After his sentence ended, he moved to Washington and began a small church in a rural part of the state. He never revealed his past record and it doesn't appear that he ever ran afoul of the law since his conversion to Jesus. Most accounts describe him as quite charismatic and his flock grew rapidly."

"'Charismatic' if you like used car salesmen," I said.

"What about his wife, Lila?" asked Jack. "She didn't appeal to Kate, either."

"She has an interesting story, too. She was born Delila Harrison in a small town in Mississippi and left as soon as she was old enough. She headed straight to Hollywood with the dream of making it as an actress or a model. The photos I've uncovered show that Lila was quite attractive when she was younger. She was able to drop her southern accent and got a few bit parts in mostly horror films. When her acting career didn't pan out as she'd hoped, she wound up working at an escort service. That career was cut short when she was arrested for illegal drug possession and dealing. Like her husband-to-be, Lila found religion when incarcerated. She also got sober and determined to turn her life around."

"How did she meet Pastor Bob?"

"Lila left the bright lights of California and moved to Washington state. She bounced from one church to another until she landed in the same rural backwoods church led by Pastor Bob. Her backstory isn't as well hidden as her husband's. After Lila and Pastor Bob were married, she began to give talks at his church about the evils of drugs and how her meeting Jesus was the beginning of her total life transformation."

"Wow, that is a lot more than I was able to dig up," Jack said.

"I also researched Richard Wycoff's background and the rest of the members of the church Board of Directors but didn't turn up anything as interesting. They are all very wealthy, but that's about it."

"What about Pastor Bob and Lila," Jack asked. "Are they wealthy?"

"I guess you could call them wealthy if their twenty-million-dollar Mercer Island waterfront home is any indication."

"They don't live in Redmond?" I asked.

"They have a spacious weekend home in Redmond, but they spend most of their time in Mercer Island when not at the church."

"Must be nice," Jack said.

"From what I can tell, Pastor Bob preaches the gospel of prosperity. The homes and his yacht—"

"He owns a yacht?" interrupted Jack.

"Their wealth is supposedly an example of what following Jesus' teachings can do for your material well-being as well as your spiritual growth."

"Sounds grand!" said Jack. "Where do I sign up?"

CHAPTER TWENTY-SIX

JACK

Richard Wycoff's DUI arrest and his murder the following day at the Holy Fellowship Church was the subject of heavy media coverage throughout the Seattle metro area. The story pushed Marie Talbot's murder investigation to the back pages of the newspapers and was barely visible on other media outlets. The social media sphere on Facebook, Twitter, and others that had been commenting and speculating about Marie's murder, now turned to Richard's. Nothing had been reported about the accounting problems at the church, which amazed Kate, given Sassy's tendency to spill all. Likewise, no one had suggested that there was a connection between the two cases. I'd contacted Detective Lucy Miller about a possible connection, but she didn't give the theory any credence, nor did the Redmond P.D. When I brought up what the church treasurer had said about the missing church funds, Miller told me that the Redmond P.D. knew about it. She wasn't on the case, so she didn't know anything more than that.

Erin had doggedly pursued a computer trail for The Holy Fellowship financial dealings but came up empty. She said that there were telltale signs that something fishy was going on, but the trail to uncover the source was well-hidden and beyond her expertise. "I can ask Bee-Bop to help if you'd like."

"What kind of name is Bee-Bop?"

"It's not his real name. Like most hackers, he goes by a handle. The name may be silly, but he's the most talented hacker I know. If anyone can hack their system, Bee-Bop is the guy. And he's very discreet. I've known him since high school. Unlike me, he wasn't caught up in that hacker crackdown." Erin got suspended from high school when she was discovered hacking into the grading system and changing her friends' grades. She had to complete 100 hours of community service and never hack again. As far as I know, she has followed all the requirements. Until now. Kate wasn't pleased that I'd asked her to use her hacking skills again, but I think Erin relished the idea. "What does this Bee-Bop guy charge for his nefarious activities?"

"That could be a problem. He's in demand now, especially for his dark web clients. He doesn't take serious risks on the cheap."

I had no idea what the dark web was all about, but it sounded sketchy at best. "Maybe you could arrange some kind of deal with him, you know, a favor for old times' sake."

"Dad, Bee-Bop is a professional hacker. He doesn't do favors."

"Well, how much does he charge?"

"I'm not sure what his going rate is now, but I'll find out."

I'd been able to snag a couple of clients, so I wasn't starving but I didn't have enough extra to spend on a "professional hacker." My savings account was almost depleted, and I needed the work, even as distasteful as the cases turned out to be. Desperate times call for desperate measures. The first case was a referral from Detective Miller about a kidnapping. At first, I thought it was a joke or prank, but she assured me it was legitimate. The police and FBI refused to take the case, however. Turns out, the kidnapped "baby" involved was a cat named Precious. The owner lived in a five thousand square foot mansion that had no signs of a break-in and she swore that she was the only one who had keys to the home. The first question that I asked was whether Precious had been eating. Erin had a lot of pets as a kid and she favored cats, so I knew a thing or two about their habits. It took me all day to search the home from top to bottom, but I found Precious. The cat, as I suspected, was sick and had hidden in an out-of-the- way space to heal. The owner was thrilled to have Precious back and immediately took her to the veterinarian to be checked out. But not before she paid my fee and added a generous bonus.

The other case was to follow a spouse and get photographic proof that he'd been cheating on his wife. The less said about that case the better. These jobs weren't at all what I thought I'd be doing when I took out a P.I. license but desperate times and all ...

Kate was busy with her own work. She'd won a contract for concierge services at a new luxury condo in Seattle that kept her on the go. With both of us working—well, she was working, I was just an embarrassed ex-homicide detective posing as a private investigator—we didn't have much time to devote to a murder investigation.

As the weeks passed, Marie Talbot's and Richard Wycoff's murders remained unsolved. Interest had started to fade, and news coverage shifted to more recent tragedies. My interest in both cases had not faded, though. After further review of Arnold DuPont's involvement, I concluded that he was a no-go as far as a suspect was concerned. The only avenue left to pursue was the Holy Fellowship Church. I was convinced that the two murders were connected. It was just a gut feeling, but I had nothing else to go on. So, I started to attend regular Sunday services. It was quite an eye opener for this old Irish Catholic boy. Other than size, the exterior was a traditional church-like structure. The interior was anything but traditional. The "chapel" resembled a huge theater, with comfortable individual seating, a state-of-the-art sound and light system, and even a performance stage instead of a pulpit. It was rock star concert ready.

On the first Sunday I attended I was greeted in the luxurious foyer by a man and woman in smart business suits. Their name tags identified them as Barry and Lily Madison, a welcoming committee of two. Experienced Walmart greeters could never match the effusive and cheery welcome this couple gave me. They immediately spotted me as a newbie and guided me straight to the

Visitor's Guest Book to sign in. They attached a name tag to my suit jacket and thrust a program in my hand.

Another church member suddenly appeared to escort me into the theater-like chapel and told me where to sit. As I sat down, I was handed a brochure about the chapel, or sanctuary, as it was called. I glanced through the brochure before the service began. It explained the significance of the many Christian symbols adorning the walls. I didn't see any statues of the Virgin Mary, but there were plenty of crosses, tapestries, and two large stone replicas of the Ten Commandments—one with cracks in it and one without. The American flag also figured prominently in the sanctuary. The brochure stated that "The United States was ordained by God and its significance is represented by the American flag."

The service started exactly on time to a full house. I found myself enjoying the high-quality, entertaining production. The worship consisted of an eclectic mix of hymns, jazz, and praise choruses, combined with biblical readings and, of course, a sermon by an enthusiastic Pastor Bob. The main takeaway from his discourse was that everyone has choices, but that each of us is responsible for what we choose. We were instructed that "You can do it, make a change, and make a difference." Pastor Bob's words were delivered powerfully. Kate didn't think Pastor Bob was charismatic, but he certainly energized the congregation.

After the closing prayer, I understood why I was asked to sit where I did. The section was reserved for first-time attendees and there were about a dozen or so of us present at the 11 o'clock service. Each was approached by a "regular" member and invited to participate in any number of church activities—from the handbell choir to Bible Study groups. I was given another pamphlet listing all the choices available. The list ran four single-spaced pages.

The second Sunday that I attended the 11 o'clock service I met Helen Benton. The church treasurer sought me out. She had been waiting for me after the service ended and introduced herself. "Call me Sassy," she said with a wink. "Everybody does."

"I know who you are," I said. "I saw you on TV."

She waved her hand as if to brush the memory away. "I was such a mess that day. Anyway, I'm glad I caught up with you. Since you're new to the Holy Fellowship you might have noticed that we don't pass an offering plate like many churches do." She handed me a business-sized envelope. We hope that you will continue to attend our services and submit a monthly donation or tithing in whatever amount you feel inspired to give."

"Thank you," I said. *I'll jump right on that.* "Speaking of finances, have you uncovered the source of the discrepancies in the church funds?"

Her eyes opened as wide as a dinner plate. "What?" She lowered her voice, "How, uh, how did you know about that?" she asked.

"I'm a private investigator," I said.

"Are you working with the police?" she asked.

"Sassy, maybe we could find a quiet, more private place to talk."

"Oh, yes. That would be best. I'll unlock my office and we can talk there."

Her office wasn't much bigger than a cubby-hole, but it was fine for my purposes. Since Sassy had a reputation for spilling the beans and probably knew more than anyone else about the people and goings on at the Holy Fellowship, I figured she'd be my best source of information. I took a few minutes to explain how I was involved in Marie Talbot's case and my belief that her murder was connected to Wycoff's.

"Really? You think the murders are connected?"

"I believe so, and what's more, I think the murderer could be someone from the Holy Fellowship."

I expected Sassy to fall off her chair with that assertion, but she surprised me. "You know, just between us chickens, I've wondered about the same thing. I mean, I don't think an outsider could have gotten into the church without being detected. We have video cameras everywhere, security guards, and an alert welcoming committee that keeps a lookout for anyone new entering the building."

"Have the police seen the video tapes from the cameras?"

"They viewed them, but the tapes were not helpful."

"What do you mean?"

"Someone had disconnected the cameras, and nothing was recorded. That's another reason I think someone in the church is involved. They'd know where and how to disconnect the cameras. You know, that's where he was killed." She pointed to an area in front of her desk. "I found him lying face down right there. There was blood everywhere. Oh, it was so horrible!"

"I can imagine."

"We had to have the whole office painted and new carpeting installed."

"Tell me about Richard Wycoff. I understand that you worked with him quite a bit."

"Yes, he was just the nicest, most respected, honest, and deeply spiritual person I've ever known."

"Hmm. I heard that he was dating Marie Talbot."

"Well, I'm embarrassed to tell you that that wasn't true, like we all thought."

"How so?"

"It was just a ruse. Marie wanted to discourage the guys from bothering her and thought that if everyone believed they were a couple that the unwanted attention would go away."

"The hoax was Marie's idea?"

"I'm not sure who dreamed it up, but it worked." She shook her head sadly. "And now they're both dead."

"Who do you think killed Richard?"

"There are a ton of rumors floating around but I can't imagine who it might be."

"What kind of rumors?"

"It's disgusting how so-called Christians are bad-mouthing Richard and Marie now."

"What are they saying?"

"Nonsense, really. One rumor is that Richard and Marie really were an item and she was pregnant with his baby. Another claims that Richard was killed by a jealous husband of a woman he'd been having an affair with. Still another rumor that's making the rounds is that Marie led a double life and wasn't the Goody-Two-Shoes that she pretended to be. Otherwise she wouldn't have been pregnant out-of-wedlock, which is what probably got her killed."

"What does your Pastor Bob say about all this rumor-mongering?"

"He's trying to put a stop to it but . . ."

"But what?"

"Please keep this confidential but the pastor's wife, Lila, has been spreading all kinds of outrageous rumors. Poor Pastor Bob. She has put him in an impossible position. She seems to get a kick out of all the rumors except when they involve her or her husband. You should have seen how upset she got when one of the rumors was that Pastor Bob and Marie had a secret romantic relationship."

"I'm sure that didn't go over well. I'd hoped to get a chance to speak to Pastor Bob, but I haven't been able to yet."

"No problem. I can introduce you. He's always delighted to meet a new member." She picked up the phone on her desk. "Let me give him a jingle. He's usually in the kitchen after the last service." She laughed. "Preaching makes him terribly thirsty and hungry." I followed Sassy to the kitchen which adhered to the "big is best" theme that the Holy Fellowship seemed to favor. The industrial-sized facility was replete with everything that any chef would need to feed the multitudes. Maybe not with just seven loaves and fishes for four thousand like in Jesus did, but certainly enough for the entire Holy Fellowship congregation.

Sassy introduced me to Pastor Bob and then excused herself. He bit into a monstrous ham sandwich with all the trimmings and gulped down a pint-size glass of iced tea. He offered to make me a sandwich and said, "There's nothing like a good ham sandwich. It's all about focusing on quality ingredients and simple techniques. Start with great bread—I prefer old-fashioned white myself—then add well-cured ham, sharp local cheese, fresh lettuce, onion, and tomato with premium mustard and voila! Perfection." He laughed as he continued to wax poetic about the greatness of ham. "I'm a natural ham myself. Most preachers need to be to perform as we do."

The sandwich he made for me was delicious as he'd promised. But for some reason, a line from the Dr. Seuss book that I used to read to Shannon kept running through my head. "*I do not like green eggs and ham. I do not like them, Sam-I-am.*" Nevertheless, our meeting was off to a good start. Breaking bread with someone always seems to make things easier to discuss. But things quickly turned awkward when a young beauty named Tanya showed up. And awkward turned explosive when the pastor's wife arrived shortly thereafter. The confrontation that ensued was more enlightening than I could have ever hoped or even prayed for.

CHAPTER TWENTY-SEVEN

KATE

Ever since I'd been awarded the contract for the newest condo in Seattle, I'd been running around town prepping for launch day like a last-minute Christmas shopper. When Erin called and asked me to come over to her place, I tried to beg off. "I'm really swamped, Erin. I've got too much to do before the grand opening of the Windmark Condo."

She wouldn't take no for an answer. Dad will be here, too," she said. "I've got some good news for both of you." My first thought was that she was pregnant again. She'd been dating a great guy for quite a while now, but I worried that it was too soon after her divorce from Rob to be getting serious. I've nothing against becoming a mother-in-law or grandmother again but I didn't think Erin was ready for a serious commitment yet. Of course, I couldn't tell her that. My disapproval would be a sure-fire excuse for her to do just the opposite. Fortunately, the news had nothing to do with marriage or babies. On the other hand, it had everything to do with marriage and babies—just in a roundabout way.

Jack bounced through the doorway like a toddler on a sugar high after too many sweets. "What are you so excited about?" I asked.

"I've been to church."

"Must have been a good sermon," Erin said, laughing. Haven't seen you that pumped for a while."

"Pastor Bob delivered an inspiring message, but it was the after party that made my day."

"After party? What are you talking about?"

"It will take some time to explain what happened. It can wait. I'm eager to hear what Erin has to tell us first."

"Let's all go into the kitchen," she said. "I've made some coffee and have some pastries from Le Panier, too." After we'd all settled in with a full mug and a French pastry, Erin began. "As you both know, I've been unable to hack the Holy Fellowship's finances. So, I turned to my friend Bee-Bop for help and he delivered."

"Wait a minute," Jack said. "I thought he wouldn't do the work without a fee. Did you convince him to give you a substantial discount?"

"I'd say it was substantial. He did it for free."

"That's great!" Jack said. "But how did you talk him into it?

"I didn't talk him into anything. When he found out that I needed info on the Holy Fellowship Church's financial dealings, he was eager to hack their system without any compensation. He even dropped everything else he was working on to do it."

Jack smiled broadly. "So, your feminine wiles did the trick after all."

"Hardly! Feminine wiles wouldn't work on Bee-Bop, particularly since they would be from the wrong gender. He has had a bad experience of some sort with the church, but he didn't go into details. I suspect it has something to do with his homosexuality. He admitted up front that he'd been a member of the megachurch at one time. According to their website, they don't accept his so-called lifestyle and believe in conversion therapy. But I really don't care what issues he had with the church. I was just thrilled that he'd agreed to the hack. He did have one condition, though."

"What was that?" I asked.

"He wants us to swear that we will never reveal his part in uncovering the church's financial malfeasance. I can't even tell you his legal name. Can we all do that?"

We agreed and she opened a folder that Bee-Bop had prepared. "According to his research, the church funds had indeed been 'siphoned off' without authorization."

"What do you mean siphoned off?" Jack asked.

"He discovered that someone had transferred large amounts of money to an account in the Cayman Islands. That account was drawn upon regularly by Marie Talbot."

"Bingo!" Jack threw both hands in the air. "So that's how she got the money for her condo and other expenses. It came courtesy of the Holy Fellowship Church."

"Did your friend Bee-Bop find out who transferred the money?" I asked.

Erin smiled. "That's the shocking part. He said the trail was well-hidden but the person to thank for the generosity is—wait for the drum roll—Pastor Bob himself."

Jack and I were speechless for a few moments. "If this is true, then the good pastor has some explaining to do," I said. "I wonder if the police have discovered the same trail."

"Maybe we should put a bug in their ear," Jack said. "I could let Detective Miller know. She'd share it with the Redmond P.D."

"No, Dad. Bee-Bop was quite clear about not passing this information on to the police."

"We could do it anonymously. Just point them in the right direction without naming names," Jack suggested.

"Bad idea. Bee-Bop is not a person we want to tangle with. He takes security breaches of his operation very seriously. I mean, scary seriously."

"Okay," I said. "Let's table your idea for a moment and talk about what this news tells us."

"What it tells me is that Pastor Bob was Marie's sugar daddy, *not* Richard Wycoff, as I first thought," Erin said.

"The pastor took advantage of a vulnerable young college student who asked for spiritual guidance and got an affair and pregnancy as a bonus," Jack snarled in disgust.

"We don't know for sure that he's the father of her baby," I said.

"Come on, Mom. This kind of stuff happens all the time. The powerful male preys on the young innocent female. All you have to do is read the newspaper or check with any other news outlet to see that it is pervasive in our society. That's what the 'Me Too' movement was all about."

"I think the drama I witnessed in the kitchen of the Holy Fellowship today can add some context to this," Jack said. He summarized his meeting with the church treasurer and their discussion of the many rumors floating around about the murder of Richard Wycoff. "Sassy said that the biggest purveyor of rumors was the pastor's wife. I got the impression that Lila has quite a temper and that was confirmed firsthand later. Sassy introduced me to Pastor Bob, who happened to be making a sandwich for himself in the church kitchen. He was very friendly and even made me a sandwich."

"Sounds like a super guy," Erin said, sarcastically. "When does the drama part of this tale start?"

"Patience, dear daughter. I'm getting to that. Anyway, Pastor Bob and I had a genial conversation, but I hadn't learned anything of real substance until a young woman named Tanya showed up. Here's how it all went down:

"Doyle?" said Pastor Bob. "I've heard that name before. Are you a friend of Sassy's?"

"No, I just met her today and—"

"I've got it!" Pastor Bob's eyes lit up like a kid at Christmas. "You're that private investigator that Richard told me about. He said you were investigating Marie's murder."

"That's right. And I'm also looking into the Richard Wycoff case. I think they may be connected."

"Oh? Are you working with the police?"

I shook my head. "No. Let's just say I have a vested interest. Marie was my daughter."

"I'm so sorry. Marie told me that she didn't know who her father was, but that she was searching for him."

"And she found me. I had no idea that she was my daughter, or that she even existed, until after she was killed."

"Bless you, my friend. That's got to be rough."

"So rough that I had a panic attack or mild shock and wound up in the ER."

"Here," he said, pouring me a glass of iced tea. You need to keep yourself hydrated." He drank some tea along with me and then added, "What else can I do for you?"

"I'd appreciate it if you would answer some questions."

"Absolutely. Ask me anything."

"I was told that Marie was dating Richard Wycoff. As you may know, she was pregnant at the time of her death. I wondered if Wycoff could be the father of my unborn grandchild."

"No, no, that's not true. We led everyone to believe that Richard and Marie were a couple. Marie was a very beautiful young woman who attracted a lot of the single guys here at Holy Fellowship. But she was also a very spiritual person who was quite dedicated to the service of Jesus Christ. She didn't want the distraction of dating anyone at the time."

"She must have been dating someone or her pregnancy was the result of an assault."

"Marie met with me for spiritual counseling, but she never mentioned that she was indeed dating anyone or that she'd been the victim of an attack. She was determined to keep and raise the baby herself."

"Why was she getting spiritual counseling?"

"Marie felt guilty over leaving the Catholic Church. I counseled her that she hadn't left her faith in Jesus, just in a form of worship that didn't work for her anymore."

"Did that help her?"

"Yes, I believe that my guidance was—"

"I'm sorry I'm late." The speaker who'd hurried breathlessly into the kitchen was a stunning young blonde with all the curves God gave her amply displayed in a low-cut white blouse over a barely-there black skirt that emphasized her tiny waist and long legs. She looked great but her attire was strikingly different from the modestly dressed women that I'd seen at the church services.

Her whirlwind entrance put a full-stop to our discussion. Pastor Bob, who'd seemed a little tired earlier, was abruptly energized. He welcomed her with an embrace that was shockingly intimate. For her part, the beauty seemed embarrassed when she realized that they were not alone. She pulled away from the pastor and said, *"Oh, I didn't know you had another meeting scheduled."*

"This is Jack Doyle, a private investigator," Pastor Bob said. *"He's just leaving."*

I took that as my cue to vacate the premises ASAP. As I headed for the door, I heard her giggle at something the pastor whispered in her ear. I had just reached for the door handle when the door was suddenly flung open. In stomped Lila, the pastor's wife 'loaded for bear' as Texas Danielle would quip. She appeared older than her husband and had begun to show a few facial wrinkles despite a heavy coat of makeup. Her attire was conservative but accented with more bling than I'd seen in some jewelry stores. *"I knew I'd find you and Tanya here,"* she said, marching up to her husband."

Pastor Bob stood in front of Tanya like a shield. *"Now, Lila, I've actually been meeting with Jack Doyle who you just about ran over storming in here."*

Lila turned and scowled at me. "Who are you?" she demanded, as if she'd not heard or paid attention to Pastor Bob's introduction.

"Jack Doyle," I repeated and handed her one of my cards.

She glanced at the card. "Oh!" she said. "Jack Doyle, the private investigator. What are you investigating?"

"The murders of Marie Talbot and Richard Wycoff," I said.

"Lila, he was just leaving."

She looked at her husband as if he'd spit on the newly waxed floor. "No, he can stay. He might be interested to hear what I have to say."

Pastor Bob left Tanya's side to escort me out. "He's a busy man."

"That's okay," I said, brushing off the pastor's reach for my arm. "I have plenty of time available today."

Lila lips turned up in a maniacal sneer. "It's always good to have a witness," she said. "Now, Bob, what exactly are you and Tanya up to? Don't tell me you're giving her counseling like you gave Marie?"

"Uh, I was just leaving, too," said Tanya. Her pale complexion had turned bright red and she was visibly shaking.

"NO!" shouted Lila. "You need to hear what I have to say, too. She darted around the pastor and squared off with the young woman. "You need to stop your so-called spiritual counseling with my husband. That means, in case you are too stupid to get my drift: STOP FUCKING MY MAN."

CHAPTER TWENTY-EIGHT

JACK

"A shouting match followed Lila's outburst. The pastor and his wife were still going at it when Tanya and I slipped out of the kitchen unnoticed."

"Wow!" said Erin. I didn't know that being a P.I. could be so entertaining. Nothing like a vulgar spat between partners to liven up a boring Sunday."

"Sounds like Pastor Bob and his wife have some issues," Kate said.

"Ya think?"

"I think we've found our killer," Erin said.

"Of whom? Marie Talbot, Richard Wycoff, or both?"

"Think of it as playing out this way," Kate suggested. "Lila was jealous of her husband's relationship with Marie and tried to stop their relationship. When she found out that Marie was pregnant—probably by Pastor Bob—she flipped out. She followed Marie to Jack's apartment on several occasions, still trying to convince her to break off with her husband. But nothing she said made a difference to Marie who had probably believed that she was in love. Or maybe she just loved the money he gave her. In any case, the day our meeting was to take place, Lila saw an opportunity to end the relationship for good. She somehow lured Marie to the roof and pushed her off."

"I have another theory," said Erin. "Pastor Bob was afraid Marie's pregnancy would become public knowledge. If it became known that Marie and Richard were *not* an item after all, questions might be raised about the nature of the pastor's 'counseling' role. If his true relationship with Marie was revealed, his standing in the church would be irreparably damaged. So, he solves the problem by killing Marie."

"Both scenarios work," I said. "Lila killed Marie just as Kate theorized or Pastor Bob was Marie's killer just as Erin suggested. But I have a different take altogether. Let's say Lila killed Marie and Pastor Bob killed Richard. Two murders and two killers."

"I suppose that's as likely as any other theory we've come up with," Kate said.

"But do we know that Pastor Bob even knew about the investigation into the church finances?" asked Erin. Didn't Mom say that Richard and the treasurer kept their investigation secret from everyone?"

"True, but Sassy has a big mouth by her own admission. Maybe she let it slip out unintentionally and Pastor Bob became alarmed enough to stop the investigation by killing Richard."

"So," said Kate. "It looks like we have several possible scenarios." She ticked them off with her fingers:

"One: Lila killed Marie.

Two: Lila killed Richard.

Three: Pastor Bob killed Marie.

Four: Pastor Bob killed Richard.

Five: Lila killed Marie and Richard.

Six: Pastor Bob killed Marie and Richard."

"There could be another scenario," said Erin. "We're wrong on all counts."

"This is when I miss being a homicide detective. If I were still on the force, I could haul both characters into the precinct and interview them properly."

"Maybe the Redmond P.D. has already done that."

My cell phone rang just then, and I checked the caller I.D. before answering. "Here we go," I said, chuckling. One of our characters is on the line." I pressed the answer button and said, "Hello, Pastor Bob." I put the phone on speaker mode so that Kate and Erin could hear our conversation.

"I'm calling to apologize for the unpleasant episode you witnessed today. Lila was totally out of line. Her use of vulgar language was particularly offensive for any Christian to hear, let alone speak. Marital difficulties should never be aired in such an inappropriate way, especially in a house of worship."

"I understand completely. Don't think anything about it." I looked at Kate and winked. "I was married to a fiery redhead. I know how some women can get themselves worked up over nothing."

"Well, anyway, you shouldn't have been exposed to our problems. Is there any way I can make it up to you?"

"As a matter of fact, there is. I'd like to talk to you again about some things that have come up since this morning."

A long pause. "Uh, what things?"

"It would be better if we could discuss them in person. Are you available to meet later today?"

"I'll tell you what. All church activities are over at 9:00 o'clock this evening. Why don't you come here around 10:00 p.m.? Everyone should have cleared out by then and we can talk without any interruptions."

"Grand! I'll see you at the church," I said, ending the call.

"Fiery redhead, huh?" Kate looked more amused than annoyed.

"Sympathizing with a suspect is a technique that works. Just a technique, Kate. Nothing more."

"Are you really going to meet the pastor tonight?" asked Erin.

"No time like the present."

"But Dad, he could be dangerous. He knows you're investigating the murders."

"Erin's right," Kate said. "Even if you got him to confess, what could you do? You don't have the authority to make an arrest anymore. And I don't think a citizen's arrest would work."

"True, but I have something else that would work."

"What's that?"

"When I got my P.I. license I used some of my meager savings to invest in some state-of-the-art equipment." I directed their attention to my lapel pin. "What do you see here?"

"An American flag. The pin is proudly worn by true patriots everywhere," said Erin, sarcastically. My daughter can be a little self-righteous at times, especially when referring to politicians or anyone else she thinks is touting their patriotism with symbols instead of actions.

"Very commonly worn, right? But this pin is actually a hidden camera. The device records video and sound. If I can get Pastor Bob to reveal anything incriminating, I will pass it on to the investigation by the police as proof and they can take it from there."

"I don't know," said Kate. "I just think it's dangerous to be confronting someone who may have murdered one or possibly two people."

"I'm not some inexperienced amateur, Kate. "I've confronted criminals before and know how to handle myself. I also have a concealed weapon permit and won't hesitate to defend myself if necessary."

We talked it over until I'd finally convinced Kate and Erin to go along with the plan I had in mind. Kate insisted that she come along with me but that she wouldn't go into the church. "Even cops ask for backup."

"Tell you what," I said. "If it will make you feel any better, I can set you up with a device so that you can hear everything that is going on. It won't have video capability but that's not really necessary."

CHAPTER TWENTY-NINE

KATE

Jack's confidence worried me. I knew that he was an experienced homicide detective, but he didn't have the full weight of the law behind him anymore. He was walking into a potentially dangerous situation with only me for backup. What a joke. About the only thing I can do is call 9-1-1 if I hear that Jack is in trouble. But I guess that's better than not being here at all. I'd be worrying even more. As much as Jack and I tangle from time to time, I still care about him. We have too much family history together to not care. He's like a pesky relative that you love but can't get rid of.

If I'd been worried before I was doubly worried when we pulled into the parking lot. There were no lights turned on inside or outside the church, which seemed foreboding. The grand structure, so magnificent during daylight hours, was grotesque in the dark, giving off an aura that screamed sinister. "The church looks deserted," I said. "Maybe Pastor

Bob changed his mind about meeting you." Jack didn't voice any such concerns.

"It's a big place," he said. "The pastor could be in his office which we can't see from here. He probably just forgot to turn on the outside lights. Don't read so much into the lack of illumination. For all we know, they take conserving energy seriously."

"Really, Jack. Energy conservation?"

"Listen, I get that you're worried but have some faith in me. I know what I'm doing, and I have a plan." He jumped out of the car after ensuring that my listening device was working properly.

"Should we have a code word or something?" I asked.

"Code word for what?"

"You know, in case you run into trouble and can't talk specifically, you could say a word that alerts me that you're in trouble."

"I think you've seen too many crime shows on TV, but okay. What word do you have in mind?"

"I don't know. Could be anything. How about Bee-Bop?" It was the first word that popped into my head and seemed innocuous enough.

Jack agreed with a patronizing smile. "Can't imagine how I'd ever work that word into a sentence, but Bee-Bop it is. Don't think I'll need to say it but if I do, call 9-1-1. Anything else before I go?"

"How will you see without lights?" I asked. "Do you even know where the pastor's office is located?"

He held up his cell phone. "I'll use the flashlight option. His office is most likely down the same hallway where the treasurer's office is."

"Please be careful, Jack," I said as he left.

"I'll be fine. One way or another, I'll get to the bottom of things tonight."

When he reached the church's front entry he said, "The door is unlocked. I'm going in now."

I mentally pictured him inside as he reported his movements. "Hello!" he shouted. "Pastor Bob? It's Jack Doyle. Are you here?" *When he didn't get an answer, he said he was heading down the hall toward the treasurer's office.* "Her office light is off, and the door is locked. There are some other small offices along this hall. I'll check them out, but it looks like there's a much larger office at the end of the hall. I'd wager good money that is where I'll find the pastor."

A moment later, he said, "Yep, it's the pastor's office, according to the gold-plated plaque attached to the door." *Jack's next words were whispered.* "I can hear voices inside the office. Sounds like Pastor Bob and his wife but I can't understand what they're saying. They aren't shouting at each other, but the tone is definitely angry." *Jack knocked on the door.* "Pastor Bob? It's Jack Doyle."

There was a long pause before the door opened. I was surprised that Lila was with the pastor, but Jack acted pleased. "Lila, how nice to see you again. I have an appointment with Pastor Bob."

"So he told me," she said. "You might as well come in and sit down. Bob said that you have some questions for him." *I pictured the seating arrangements—the pastor probably sat behind an executive desk, Lila in a guest chair alongside him and Jack in another guest chair facing them. I imagined that the pastor's office was several magnitudes nicer in décor and comfortable furnishings than Sassy's cubby-hole had been.*

"Actually, it's grand that you're here as well, Lila," Jack said. "Maybe you can shed light on some other questions I have."

"Go ahead, Mr. Doyle. We're happy to assist you in your investigation." *Despite the pastor's open manner, I detected a tense undercurrent in the room. Lila's greeting was perfunctory rather than welcoming.*

"Pastor Bob, I've been told that Richard Wycoff and your treasurer, Sassy Benton, had been investigating the possible embezzlement of church funds. Were you aware of their investigation?"

"I can answer that," said Lila. "We both knew what they were up to. They were on a fishing expedition and found nothing untoward."

"Would it surprise you that, in fact, their investigation wasn't without merit?"

"What do you mean?" asked Lila. *I found it interesting that she was doing most of the talking so far.*

"It so happens that I have proof from a reliable source who is a computer genius. He skillfully accessed your church's financial records even though it was a complicated trail. He discovered that funds had been diverted from official church accounts to an offshore account in the Cayman Islands."

"That's preposterous!" *Pastor Bob's voice sounded more nervous than outraged.* "No one from Holy Fellowship would engage in such a dishonest act."

"The documents my source recovered say otherwise. In fact, they show that the person who authorized the funds transfer was none other than yourself, Pastor. And, what's more, the Cayman Island account was regularly accessed by Marie Talbot."

"You motherfucker!" shouted Lila. "You told me that those funds were for us! Our protected 'go-to' bankroll in case things turned tits up." *Her coarse language startled me more than her admission.*

"I . . . uh, I can explain," stuttered Pastor Bob.

"No, Bob, let me explain things to you," said Lila. *Her tone was deliberate and forceful.* "I've had enough of your fooling around with all the pretty young things that you take under your counseling wing. Marie is gone but you have Tanya all primed and ready to step into her shoes. Only that's not going to happen this time. Those funds will *not* go to Tanya. They will be transferred into *my* personal account where I can keep a close watch on them."

"Here's something else to consider," said Jack. "I've seen all kinds of motives for murder during my fifteen years as a homicide detective. The top three are money, love, and revenge. Richard Wycoff's murder was probably related to his investigation of the financial scheme. The disclosure of financial impropriety is a top motive for murder, in my book."

"Are you implying that one of us killed Richard?" asked Lila.

"Well, it has occurred to me. Did you kill him?"

"Of course not!" said Pastor Bob. "Your allegations are absurd. We won't answer any more of your questions. This meeting is over." *I was relieved to hear him say that. I wanted Jack out of there as soon as possible.*

"No, it's not over," insisted Lila. "Let the man talk. I want to hear what else he's dreamed up about us."

"Fine by me," Jack said. "I believe that your husband was having an affair with Marie Talbot. You just confirmed it. The records show that he had been subsidizing her lifestyle with the embezzled church funds. I also believe that he was most likely the father of her unborn child. The way I see it, the pastor of a major church has a lot to lose if his affair with a young parishioner who's carrying his child becomes public."

"What? Now you're suggesting that I killed Marie?" asked the pastor.

"Not necessarily. Your wife could have killed her. Jealousy falls under the heading of love gone wrong. One of the top three motives."

"Jealous, my ass! I wasn't jealous of that slut. Tell him, Bob. Tell him why I had to get rid of her."

"No, please, Lila. Don't do it. He's just fishing."

"Shut up! I've known all about our dear pastor's sexual proclivities for years now and really don't give a damn. But I very much care if the rest of our congregation found out. The scandal would seriously jeopardize the lifestyle that we've come to enjoy. Bob and Marie could've kept their affair going if no one knew, but her pregnancy changed everything. The truth would eventually come out. So, naturally I had to end things once and for all. I just carried out what needed to be done. If Marie had gone through with what she'd promised, she'd still be alive today."

I couldn't believe it. Jack got a confession!

"What did Marie promise to do?" asked Jack.

"She agreed to an abortion," admitted the pastor.

"I thought the church was opposed to abortion," Jack said. "Your church held regular protests at Planned Parenthood."

"There are certain compromises one must make from time to time," said Pastor Bob.

"Call us hypocrites if you must," said Lila, "but Marie was too holier-than-thou to take care of the problem. So, I took care of it for her."

There was a brief pause and some noise that I couldn't identify. "Whoa!" said Jack. His outburst was followed by Pastor Bob shouting, "What are you doing, Lila?"

"Taking out an insurance policy. It appears that our house of cards is about to come crashing down. If this wannabe detective starts spreading his accusations and so-called proof to the right audience, we're done for. The cops haven't got a clue, but that could change if he can convince them he's right."

"But we don't know that he has proof of anything. This is all a clever trick to get us to confess. Put the gun away!"

Oh my God! She has a gun. Say the code word NOW, Jack! Bee-Bop! Bee-Bop!

"Hold on, Lila," Jack said. I didn't come here tonight to trick either of you into a confession. I came here to offer you a proposition that would be beneficial to all of us."

"What did you have in mind? And make it quick."

"I became a P.I. because I got unjustly thrown off the police force. Believe me, I'm no fan of the thin blue line. A crooked Seattle detective is responsible for my current situation."

"What situation?"

"I'm dead broke and my P.I. business is going nowhere. I'm not proud to admit this, but it explains why I'm offering a way out of the troubles we both face. My proposition is simply this: I'll destroy all the documentation that I have proving Pastor Bob's embezzlement and true relationship with Marie Talbot. I will also keep quiet about Lila's murder of Marie Talbot if you will—"

"Here it comes," quipped Pastor Bob. Doyle's nothing but a low-down blackmailer."

"I prefer to think that I'm a kindred spirit. We each appreciate the type of life that wealth can provide. I just want my own piece of the pie."

"What kind of pie are we discussing here?" asked Lila.

"You authorize a transfer of the Cayman Island funds to me. I'm not greedy. I only want half. That leaves you with plenty of 'go to' cash, as you called it, if you need to disappear for any reason. Here's my bank account's routing number."

Blackmail? That's Jack's plan? He'd gotten a confession from Lila, but he'd incriminated himself in the whole sordid mess to do it. Would the police believe it was a bluff or a sincere offer? This plan doesn't sound good to me at all.

"No way!" shouted the pastor. "He knows nothing. This is all just a bluff."

"Shut up, Bob! Think about it. Doyle's offering us an escape plan. If he figured out what we've done, the police will eventually come to the same conclusions. It's time to shit or get off the pot, dear hubby. Are you in or not? she asked.

An unbearable deafening silence followed. It was probably only ten seconds, but it felt like an eternity. Lila broke the silence. "Too late," she said.

A loud bang exploded in my ear. Oh, my God! Who'd she shoot? I had my finger on the last digit to call 9-1-1 when Lila said, "Well, that takes care of one problem. Now it's your turn, Mr. Pie-Eater."

What's did she mean? Was she going to shoot Jack? Do I wait for the code word? I was so nervous that I couldn't think straight. Jack was in trouble and there was no time to wait for a code word. I pressed the last digit to call 9-1-1 and jumped out of the car. My heart was beating so hard I thought I might pass out. I was so breathless that I could hardly talk to the operator. I'm not sure if I even said the words or just thought them. "Send the police! Someone's been shot at the Holy Fellowship Church. Hurry!"

I could still hear Lila talking as I raced into the church which gave me hope that I wasn't too late. Maybe I could distract her before she shot Jack. I ran down the hall energized by sheer terror. All I knew was that Jack needed me. He could be dead by the time the police arrived. The fact that I could be dead too never even entered my mind.

When I burst into the room, I saw everything in a split second. Lila and Jack stood facing each other. Pastor Bob was slumped in his chair with a bloody hole in his forehead. Lila had a monster gun in her left hand. I didn't have time to think about the terrifying sight or the danger her gun posed. Fight or flight hormones raged through my body. I always thought I'd freeze in a life or death moment, but I reacted instinctively and instantly. I crouched low to the floor like a wild animal preparing to pounce on its prey and launched myself at Lila. She yelped but I think I'd startled her more than frightened her.

Jack yelled, "Kate! NO!" But he was too late. I tackled Lila around her waist and we both fell to the floor. I landed on top of her right side and her gun was pinned underneath her left side. Lila was stronger than she looked, and she easily tossed me off her. All I'd managed to do was grab one of her gold necklaces and break it. Jack pulled me out of her reach just as Lila drew her weapon. Another loud bang. Now Jack was on the floor and bleeding. "Get out, Kate!" he groaned.

There was no way I'd leave Jack. His suit jacket was drenched in blood but the holster for his service weapon was open and within my reach. Panic-stricken and heart beating in my chest so hard that it felt like it would explode, I inched my hand nearer to his gun.

But Lila had already aimed her gun at me. "Freeze!" she yelled. "Don't even try it!" Staring down the barrel of a gun was the most terrifying sight I'd ever experienced. Sirens blared in the distance. I reacted as if our rescuers could hear me. "BEE-BOP!! BEE-BOP!! BEE-BOP!"

The words I kept screaming seemed to confuse Lila. When she hesitated, I took a chance. I scrambled toward her and jumped on top of her again. Credit the massive amount of adrenalin surging through my body, divine intervention, or just plain luck but somehow, I got my hands on her gun. We both tugged for control for several gut-wrenching seconds which seemed like hours. Her finger was still on the trigger and she got off a shot that hit the chandelier above us. I grabbed at her gun again as shattered crystal rained down upon us. Another loud bang exploded. The pain in my chest left me breathless.

The last thing I saw was Jack's frantic face. He was still on the floor but had managed to draw his own weapon. Then he fired. Everything went black after that.

CHAPTER THIRTY

A DAUGHTER'S PERSPECTIVE

When I first learned that my father had another daughter whom he didn't even know existed and that she'd been murdered, I was furious with him. I was also furious with my mother. If she hadn't kicked him out of the house in the first place, he'd never have taken up with some random woman in a bar. Why couldn't they stay married? After they divorced, I never gave up hope that they'd someday get back together. It wasn't until I got divorced myself that I understood how relationships can change over time and no longer work.

Circumstances beyond our control often happen and force change upon us. My parents, like many others, have had to make career changes. Through no fault of their own, Mom and Dad both lost their chosen careers and had to start over with varying degrees of success. They are resilient and resourceful people. I like to think that I have inherited those same traits.

Dad has never given up on reuniting with Mom and I have supported his efforts. I still believe after all these years that they belong together. Mom wasn't as convinced but she always stood by Dad and helped him when she could. So, it wasn't all that surprising to me that she would volunteer to help Dad with his first case as a private investigator. I tried to discourage her because I thought a murder investigation was dangerous and exposed her to a risk that she didn't need to take. But take it she did and now all our lives have changed. I even found myself wrapped up in the investigation, although my participation never posed any risks to my personal safety. I consider myself a purpose-driven individual. Give me a problem to solve and I jump right in. I think that is another trait that I inherited from my parents. True or not, it does explain my involvement.

Sometimes all that stands between a functioning society and chaos is the desire and ability of those who step up and take charge. A respected member of the community and his wife had become the antithesis of all that they supposedly believed and taught. Their misdeeds resulted in murders, grievous injuries, and tremendous loss. The scandal at the Holy Fellowship Church made national news and generated prolific media coverage. And my parents were at the heart of it all. They'd stepped up and solved a case at great risk to themselves. Offers for print and TV interviews and even a book deal were discussed, but they declined. I think they were embarrassed by all the fuss. Mom admitted that she was tempted to agree to the interview request from Oprah Winfrey (she was a fan) but she turned her down, too.

My parents' strength and resilience have been severely tested but overall, I think they are better people for the experience they've been through. Mom and Dad both sustained serious injuries but received expert medical care and have fully recovered. We can even joke now about how Mom charged to Dad's rescue like a mother bear protecting her cubs, yelling "Bee-Bop! Bee-Bop!" Although injured himself, Dad was able to wound and disarm the pastor's wife. He kept her subdued until the police arrived shortly thereafter. She has been charged with three counts of murder—Marie's, Richard's, and Pastor Bob's. She confessed that she murdered Richard Wycoff to stop his financial investigation and would have killed her husband sooner had she known that he'd been giving Marie Talbot the funds. The prosecutor is on record as saying he has a slam-dunk case for her conviction. Embezzlement charges against her were considered but dropped when police investigators discovered account documents that proved Pastor Bob was responsible. Bee-Bop's role was never revealed. The video and sound recording that Mom was afraid would implicate Dad in a blackmail scheme was dismissed as irrelevant by the prosecutor. He used the recording as evidence against Lila and Pastor Bob. The Cayman Island accounts were transferred back to the church, along with the proceeds from the couple's assets that were sold at auction.

Some people expected that, in the aftermath of the scandal, attendance at the Holy Fellowship would suffer and the church would eventually have to disband. The opposite occurred. Attendance soared. Reasons varied, depending on who you talked to. Mom's view is that true faith can be jolted from time to time but never destroyed.

Dad's nemesis, Detective Kevin Gleason, was fired from the Seattle Police Department after an extensive Internal Affairs review. Besides planting evidence against Dad, he was accused of sexual harassment by his partner, Detective

Lucy Miller. The firing left an opening in the homicide unit. Lucy said Dad should apply for Gleason's old position. She said it would be poetic justice. Dad thought about it—he really missed working as a homicide detective—but passed on the opportunity. I think he was influenced by how well his private investigator business was doing due to all the good publicity he'd received. He happily admits that he's been so busy that he is considering hiring an associate. I volunteered, but he said that he'd sooner hire Kevin Gleason before he'd hire his daughter.

Mom's injuries healed fast but Dad's guilt over involving her in the case are ongoing. Mom said she feels guilty over how her impulsive action was what put them both in danger. Lila had just agreed to Dad's blackmail proposal when Mom burst into the room and tackled her. In the ensuing struggle, her gun fired and wounded Mom and Dad. Their feelings about guilt reminded me of a line that I read in a novel by Sabaa Tahir. "There are two kinds of guilt: the kind that drowns you until you're useless, and the kind that fires your soul to purpose." I believe that my parents will eventually heal with a renewed sense of purpose.

What has already healed, though, is their relationship. Mom says that their experience made her realize just how much she loves Dad. They aren't ready to re-marry but, as their friend Danielle says, "The fire is red hot."

THE END

ABOUT THE AUTHOR

Valerie Wilcox received a master's degree in Education from the University of Oregon and is a former educator and employee development specialist. She currently lives in Vancouver, Washington and when not writing, can often be found walking her two dogs at Ft. Vancouver.

OTHER NOVELS BY VALERIE WILCOX

NOTE FROM THE AUTHOR

Word-of-mouth is crucial for any author to succeed. If you enjoyed the book, please leave a review online—anywhere you are able. Even if it's just a sentence or two. It would make all the difference and would be very much appreciated.

Thanks!
Valerie

Thank you so much for reading one of our
Mystery novels.
If you enjoyed our book, please check out our
recommendation for your next great read!

K-Town Confidential by Brad Chisholm and Claire Kim

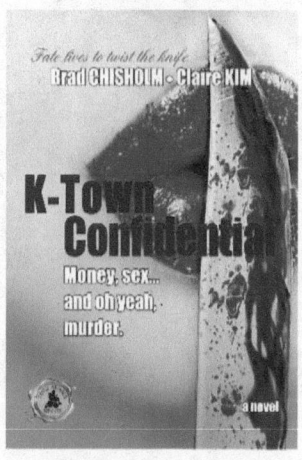

"An enjoyable zigzagging plot."
–Kirkus Reviews

"If you are a fan of crime stories and legal dramas that
have a noir flavor, you won't be disappointed with *K-
Town Confidential*."
–Authors Reading